THE *Ghost*
OF SHEPPARD'S INN

INDIGORIVER
PUBLISHING

Ghost THE

OF SHEPPARD'S INN

M. DAVID

Indigo River Publishing

Indigo River Publishing
3 West Garden Street Ste. 352 M
Pensacola, FL 32502
www.indigoriverpublishing.com

Book Design: mycustombookcover.com
Editor: Earl Tillinghast, Regina Cornell

Ordering Information: Quantity sales: Special discounts are available on quantity purchases by corporations, associations, and others. For details, contact the publisher at the address above.

Orders by U.S. trade bookstores and wholesalers: Please contact the publisher at the address above.

Printed in the United States of America

Library of Congress Control Number: 2019943544

ISBN: 978-1-948080-97-2

First Edition

With Indigo River Publishing, you can always expect great books, strong voices, and meaningful messages. Most importantly, you'll always find ... words worth reading.

Dedication

I dedicate this book to my wife, Sharon; our family; and the wonderful caregivers who help the "forgotten generation" of loving elderly people residing in assisted-living and mental-care facilities.

Friends often ask me about the origins of my stories. *The Ghost of Sheppard's Inn* came from my heart. Although fiction, it is based on reality. Sharon's mom, Lillian (my mother-in-law), spent the end of her life in a facility where she was cared for by the comforting staff, as well as by Sharon, her loving daughter. We were blessed to meet many truly amazing people, including Angelina, a living angel, who loved Lillian as her own family.

Why a ghost story? I can't tell you that ghosts are real, but I can say that the relationship between my father, Bill, and my mother, Shirley, was undeniably special. They spent most of their lives dancing like Fred Astaire and Ginger Rogers. When mom passed, my dad's relationship with Lillian grew to a point where they became best friends.

In case you were wondering, Lillian loved to be called Diamond Lil, and Bill was known as an honest car salesman who drove a big gold Lincoln Continental!

PROLOGUE

AT TWO IN THE MORNING, ALL THE RESIDENTS WERE IN THEIR ROOMS
AND SAFELY TUCKED INTO THEIR BEDS. The sounds of snoring slipped
under the doors and melodically flowed into the hallways. Even the
staff felt drowsy as they sat in their offices, filling out medical forms and
creating rosters for the next day's activities.

A sudden chill slowly worked its way from the elevator at the end
of the hall and caused the normal seventy-degree temperature to drop.
The smell in the air turned foul, the lights flickered off, and the sound
of snoring was soon replaced by an indescribable screeching.

The staff and residents succumbed to a deep sleep with little
possibility of waking to see what was happening. The nightmare was
beginning!

One by one, doors to the individual rooms were opened and
the residents examined to insure they remained in their coma-like
condition. The drawers on the night tables and dressers were quietly
opened. Items were removed and examined thoroughly. Some were
taken, others replaced, and then the drawers were gently closed.

Pictures were pulled from the walls and remounted on their hooks
moments later. The televisions were next. They were lifted off their
bases and put on the floor. The cable-box wiring and connections were
reconfigured. Then everything else was put back the way it had been.

It didn't take long to move from one room to the next. Whatever
was missed would be discovered at another time. There were four floors

of rooms to search and only a few hours left before everyone came back to life.

At five in the morning the air in the hallways slowly returned to the proper temperature. The ungodly screeching slowly began to fade. The lights throughout the building flickered back on. The foul odor diminished and was replaced by fresh-smelling air, and the gentle sounds of snoring could once again be heard.

Another nightmare had ended, and Sheppard's Inn returned to normal.

CHAPTER ONE

FRIGID AIR EMBRACED THE SIMMONS FAMILY AS THEY SLOWLY EXITED THE CAR. The weather was a lot colder than what they had experienced on the cruise ship. It was only twenty feet to the large automatic double doors that allowed entry to the small foyer of Sheppard's Inn. Yet walking the remaining twenty feet could quickly cause a person to freeze to death.

Adam's father had to once again remind his son that they could no longer use their real last name.

"We're the Smiths now. I'm Jack Smith, your mom is Carol Smith, and you're Adam Smith. Don't slip up. It's important for you to remember that the Simmons family no longer exists. Our lives depend on keeping incognito!"

Adam replied sarcastically, "Gee, could you pick a more common name? I would have liked to be called Adam Aardvark. It has a nice ring to it, don't you think?"

Adam's mom chuckled and said, "Adam Aardvark is wonderful, son, but that would make me Carol Aardvark, and that sounds terrible. Let's stick to Smith. Oh, by the way, I'm not just your mother; I'm also your teacher. You may not be able to formally attend school, but you will still be continuing your classes, young man."

The reality was that the Simmons family had ceased to exist the day their home was set on fire by Tony the Match.

The Simmons family had sprung a trap that had placed Tony and his mob boss in jail for a very long time. Everyone in their hometown of Huntingdon Valley, including the mobsters from Philadelphia, believed that Jack, Carol, and Adam had died in the house fire. The police were provided with evidence to prove it. Because of the efforts of Adam and his family, illegal drugs were no longer on the streets or in the schools of the little town of Huntingdon Valley, where they once lived. The head of a drug-dealing mob and a dangerous arsonist were now behind bars.

Like a good magic trick, the Simmons family had just disappeared in a puff of smoke.

...

After slipping away and spending two weeks cruising the Caribbean, it was time for the family formerly known as the Simmons to rejoin society, which now happened to be in Denver, Colorado. It took Adam's dad some creative effort and truth stretching to fill out the employment forms he had obtained online from Sheppard's Inn. To his surprise, it had worked. Jack Smith was hired as a maintenance man. His wife, a great cook with impeccably contrived references, was immediately chosen as the new executive chef. Besides being homeschooled, Adam would spend time volunteering to entertain the elderly residents.

Adam shivered as he removed the multiple suitcases from the car and placed them on the ground.

"Hey, do I get my own room?" he asked.

"You're lucky if you get your own bed," his dad replied.

Both doors automatically opened as they approached the entrance, and the sudden blast from the foyer's ceiling heater instantly warmed their chilled bones. Ten feet from the entry foyer sat a man at a little reception desk. The bright overhead fluorescent lights of the foyer threw harsh shadows across the man's face. Grayish hair framed his ears, his eyebrows were straggly, and his dry lips protruded in front of his drawn cheeks. On his skeleton-like frame he wore an ill-fitting green sweater that was embroidered with a Sheppard's Inn patch.

After many attempts he slowly rose from the chair and extended his hand. His creaking bones created sounds that competed with his soft, raspy voice. He managed to utter, "Hello, my name is Ivan. Welcome to Sheppard's Inn. I hope you enjoy your stay." He pointed to the corner. "You can use that."

CHAPTER TWO

GRABBING THE RICKETY LUGGAGE CART THAT STOOD IN THE SHADOWS OF THE LOBBY'S CORNER, ADAM'S FATHER STRUGGLED TO MANEUVER IT OUTSIDE TO THE CAR. Appearing to be in worse shape than Ivan's body, its bad wheels squeaked in protest while rolling across the cold concrete walkway. Accompanying his father back to the frigid outdoors, Adam felt pain in his fingers, which began to ache as they quickly succumbed to the icy cold. Worried about frostbite, he rapidly removed the bags from the car and loaded them haphazardly on the cart. With his father's help, it only took a few minutes to manhandle the now-overloaded squeaking cart on its return trip to the foyer.

Once back into the comforting warmth of the foyer, the family approached the front desk. Ivan the skeleton man reached out once again to shake hands. "You and your wife will be staying in room B1, and you"—he cackled as he pointed to Adam with a bony, crooked finger—"will be staying in room B2."

Adam, with a forced smile, didn't care about this strange man or his bony finger. He silently rejoiced that he had his own room. Now all he needed was a television and his life would be perfect!

"Your rooms are in the basement. But don't worry; there are no more bedbugs. There's no guarantee about the spiders, though."

Bedbugs? Spiders? Is this weird guy serious? Adam thought.

"Oh, by the way. You're not afraid of ghosts, are you?"

"Ghosts?" Adam replied weakly.

The old man coughed and laughed as he pointed the way to the elevator. "Sleep tight and don't let the bedbugs bite!" he shouted.

That was the last thing Adam and his family wanted to hear as they entered the elevator.

...

It took an agonizing three minutes for the elevator to arrive at the basement level.

"Hey, we only went down one floor. Why did it take so long?"

"Must be the spiderwebs in the elevator shaft slowing things down," his mother answered.

"Very funny! My mom is not only a drama teacher, she's also a comedian," Adam stated.

"Here's our room—room B1," Adam's father said as he opened the creaking door.

The room was not very spacious. It had a queen-size bed, two dressers, no windows, and a small, ancient tube-style television sitting on a little metal stand.

Adam's father handed him a key. "Go check out your room."

Twenty feet down the hall was a door with a crooked little sign that read B2.

Please have a TV. I don't care if it's an old tube unit made in the eighties. Please have a TV, Adam kept praying as he unlocked the door.

The room was more like a large closet than a bedroom. Dirty white paint was peeling off the walls, old blackened pipes lined the ceiling, and a dresser sat so close to the small twin bed that navigating around the room would be a real challenge. And of course there was no trace of a TV. Adam groaned loudly. He was not a happy camper.

"What's wrong?" his father asked as he peeked into Adam's tiny room.

Adam shouted, "It's a dump, a smelly, dirty dump of a closet with no TV!"

"All it needs is a little paint and it will be a palace," his dad chuckled.

The black overhead pipes started to rattle, years of accumulated dust drifted down from above, and suddenly a big spider dropped onto Adam's shoulder. In shock, Adam jumped back and quickly brushed the spider away.

"A little paint! Is that what you think?" Adam replied in anger.

Suddenly there was a strange creaking sound. The lights started to flicker, and the room became cold!

"I think we're going to need a little more than paint," Adam moaned. "Can I sleep with you guys tonight?"

"Sure, son," his father replied. "It's probably better than sleeping in a room with a ghost."

A slight look of concern crept across his dad's face as Adam reached for his hand as they walked back to room B1.

...

Later that evening, Adam's dad lay on the bed with his wife sleeping on the right and his snoring son on the left. He couldn't help but think, *Am I once again putting my family in danger?* He closed his eyes and drifted to sleep.

In the distance the strange creaking sound began to fade.

Chapter Three

THE FOLLOWING DAY'S AGENDA INDICATED THAT THE SMITH FAMILY SHOULD BE AT THE MAIN DINING ROOM NO LATER THAN SEVEN IN THE MORNING. Jack and Carol couldn't wait to begin their new jobs. Adam, on the other hand, was cautiously optimistic. He tossed and turned in his sleep while dreaming of his harrowing adventures in Huntingdon Valley, how he had searched for his kidnapped friends, and what he had found at Gold's Funeral Home. The nightmare of seeing a dead person with bulging eyes continued to haunt him.

The bright, cheery atmosphere of the main dining room automatically placed everyone in a good mood. Although quite large, it had a cozy appeal. Scattered about were thirty round tables that could individually seat up to eight diners. The tables were covered with tablecloths in assorted pastel colors, and each had a glass vase containing freshly cut flowers.

Sitting at a rear table, well out of earshot of anyone passing by, were Adam and his parents.

"This coffee is pretty good," his dad said to his mom. "But the scrambled eggs are terrible."

"I guess that's why they hired me as a cook," his mom replied. She winked at her husband. "I only hope I can live up to the great résumé you created about my incredible cooking skills."

"Don't worry, dear," his dad replied. "I have confidence in you."

"Yeah, mom, your cooking was a hit in Huntingdon Valley. It was life changing for—"

"Shush," his mother replied. "Remember, we have new lives now!"

His dad threw him a reprimanding look and reminded them to keep their voices down.

His mother continued: "As an executive chef I have to come up with healthy dishes that taste great. Older people shouldn't have too much salt in their diets. That doesn't mean their food should be bland. There are other spices besides salt that I can use to make their food delicious."

Adam had total confidence in his mom's cooking abilities. After all, her famous sauce and meatballs were the reason that Tony the Match and his boss had been easily apprehended. Her extra added ingredients made the difference. The police had found the arsonist and his boss sitting at the table, slumped over, with their faces submerged in a bowl of meatballs and sauce. Mom's cooking made everyone happy that day. That is, everyone except the mob boss and his arsonist employee—for them it was life changing!

"What's my job at this place?" Adam asked.

"Socialize with the residents and maybe catch a ghost," his father replied.

"A ghost? Seriously? Is there something going on around here that you're not telling me about? Is this place haunted?"

His dad smiled. "Only if the rumors are true."

Adam thought back to what he had seen in the movies: vampires, zombies, and poltergeists. This was not good, not good at all! Were ghosts real?

"Are we in any danger?"

"Well, son, I guess that depends on the ghost."

Adam couldn't tell if his father was serious or just having a little fun.

"You know, it was bad enough when I was chased by mobsters, and now you're telling me that this place is haunted?"

"Maybe it is, maybe it isn't," his dad replied.

"Great, just great!"

Chapter Four

After breakfast Adam and his mom took a guided tour of the facility, beginning with the large commercial-style kitchen containing an assortment of gleaming top-of-the-line stainless-steel appliances. The twelve-burner oven with cast-iron grates sat next to an oversized double fryer. Two double-deck convection ovens stood waiting to do their jobs. It was a chef's dream.

Leaving his family in good hands, Dad searched for the maintenance department, which was located in the sub-basement level.

"This place is a lot bigger than I thought," he mumbled to himself as he stepped off the elevator and began his exploration of the sub-basement's halls. There was a machine shop filled with drill presses, band saws, and other woodworking equipment; a mechanical shop containing pumps of all sizes; an electrical room lined with large wall-mounted circuit-breaker panels; and a security room with an array of CCTV recorders and large-screen monitors. There was even a room that housed all sizes of oxygen tanks and other medical devices.

Suddenly Jack felt something touch his shoulder. He jumped and quickly turned around, hoping he wouldn't have to deal with a giant spider.

"Are you lost?" asked a man dressed in blue ill-fitting overalls. "You look like you've seen a ghost!"

"Sorry about that. I just didn't hear you coming. I recently had a conversation with my boy about ghosts, and I guess I'm a little jumpy."

The man smiled. "My name is Stu, and you are?"

"Jack, Jack Smith. This is my first day. I was just hired as the new maintenance man."

"Well, then we have somethin' in common. I'm the *old* maintenance man."

They shook hands.

"Hmm, you don't look like a Jack Smith. I knew a Jack Smith once, and you don't look like him at all."

Jack smiled and quickly responded, "I didn't catch your last name. What was it again?"

Stu took a deep breath. "Majeboffski. Stuart Majeboffski!"

"That's one heck of a name. I bet you had some problems going through school with that name. Wow, can you imagine having that name on the back of a football jersey? That's almost as bad as Ben Roethlisberger."

Stu laughed. "When my parents first came to this country they were advised to shorten it to Jeboff, but they never did. After sixty-eight years I kinda got used to it."

"Well, it's a pleasure to meet you, Stuart."

"Please call me Stu. Stuart is way too long."

They both laughed.

"Follow me, Jack. Let me show ya my humble abode."

"So tell me, Stu, why are you leaving? Better yet, what made you take this job in the first place?"

"Well, that's a long story, Jack. I sold medical equipment in the New York area for more than forty years. I was pretty good at it too. One day enough was enough. I had a long phone conversation with my niece Rebecca, who's the social director here. She told me that Sheppard's Inn was a great place to work. Next thing you know, my wife and I sold the house, came here, and for the past three years my wife has been freezin' to death. She can't stand the cold! She has accumulated more sweaters than a supermodel has bikinis."

"Did your wife have a job?"

"Yep, she was a microbiologist. Come to think of it, she still is a microbiologist. She just doesn't get paid for it anymore!"

"She sounds like a smart lady!"

"Yep. She's smart enough to know that someplace warm is where we should live the rest of our lives. She's been buggin' me for over a year to move. So goodbye, Colorado; hello, Florida!"

"I have to ask you, Stu, why does everyone here believe that this place is haunted?"

Stu's left eyebrow lifted as he replied, "When it comes to ghosts I'm pretty skeptical, but I have to tell you, there are a lot of strange things goin' on around here!"

Now Jack was intrigued. "What kind of strange things?"

They both took a seat at Stu's metal worktable.

"People swear that the temperature drops in the middle of the night. They complain about ungodly, strange noises. There's this lingerin' odor, which could be making people sick. The lights are flickerin' and going off. And to top it off, things are disappearin'!"

"Disappearing?" Jack asked. "Many of the residents have memory issues. Maybe some of their items are just being misplaced."

"Yep, that's what I think, Jack, but I have to tell you, ever since Diamond Bill died, things have been getting pretty spooky around here!"

"Diamond Bill? Who was he?"

"Just one of the nicest people you'd ever meet," Stu replied. "He had the reputation of being the most honest car salesman that ever lived. He was a snappy dresser who walked around wearin' his wife's diamond ring on his pinky finger. She died a few years before Diamond Bill. He would always talk about her to anyone who would listen. People tell me that Bill and his wife could light up a room. He could always tell a good joke, and she was a little red-haired firecracker that could make a sailor blush. He loved her so much, and her ring was the only thing he had left. He cherished it as much as he cherished her."

The telephone rang and Stu quickly answered it.

"That was the memory care unit. They seem to have a problem

with the oxygen tanks. They were pretty frantic on the phone. Come on, Jack; let's pick up some fresh tanks and hurry up there.

Chapter Five

"This is the kitchen where you'll be working," Rebecca pointed out to Adam's mom. "If you don't mind, I'll drop you off here and continue Adam's tour to the memory care unit."

Adam accompanied Rebecca out of the dining room and into the long hallway that was congested with older people moving about. She explained her duties of being the social director, which ranged from creating events to interacting with the residents. As they walked, Adam realized that just about every resident was in a wheelchair or was using a cane or walker.

"Are all these people sick?" he asked.

"Some," Rebecca replied. "But mostly they're in pain. They have arthritis, bad hearts, and back problems. That's what happens when you get old, especially when you don't take care of yourself when you are young."

Adam began to realize that eating a SuperBurger and fries might one day put him in a wheelchair. *I wonder, if other kids knew about this, would they consider changing their eating habits?*

"You said we were going to the memory care unit. What's that?" he asked.

"A memory care unit? I said that?" Rebecca replied.

Adam was confused.

Rebecca laughed. "I'm just joking. When you work here you have to try to keep a happy face and a good sense of humor. Dealing with the ghost doesn't make it easier, but that's a whole other story. We better get going before I forget where it is!"

Adam didn't know if she was talking about the location of the memory care unit or the location of the ghost. People around here seemed to be friendly, but they were also very strange. Was there really a ghost haunting Sheppard's Inn?

...

"Help. *Help!* We need some help here!" came from the distance.
"We better hurry," Rebecca said to Adam as she grabbed his hand and started to run.

"What's going on?" Adam asked.

"It's the memory care unit. One of the patients must have fallen. It's happening again. Ever since Diamond Bill died . . ." Rebecca became breathless as they continued to run.

"Who's Diamond Bill?" Adam asked.

"You'll find out soon enough. Right now we have to pick up the pace!"

Within minutes they approached the double metals doors of the memory care unit. Adam proceeded to push the door on the right side, but it wouldn't open.

"You need this," Rebecca said as she waved a small card at the little black box located near the side of the door. The red light on the box turned green. "It's a proximity reader, which disengages the magnetic lock. Now press the big square button on the wall."

The door automatically opened.

"Wow, that's some security system you have here," Adam remarked.

Rebecca smiled. "It doesn't seem to stop a ghost!" She pushed Adam through the open door. "In that room over there."

Three of the staff were attempting to lift an older woman off the floor and back onto her bed.

"It's Lilly," they explained to Rebecca. "She fell again. That's the third time this month!"

Adam stood in the background as one of the staff medically examined Lilly while the other checked her vital signs. Her blood pressure appeared elevated, her pupils slow to respond, and her eyes were glazed.

"Lilly, are you okay?" they kept asking.

During the few minutes it took for Lilly to finally respond, a nasty bluish-green bump began to form on her forehead. Her eyes opened slightly, and she managed a quiet whisper.

"The ghost was here. The ring, Bill's ring—you have to find it!" She then closed her eyes, and her breathing slowed.

"Is she dead?" Adam asked in a shaky voice.

They put a stethoscope on her chest. "No, she's in shock. Her heart is weak, but she's still with us. We're going to need a doctor to look at that bump."

Adam breathed a sigh of relief and thought to himself, *Thank you, God! I couldn't take seeing a person die before my eyes. Now, about this ring and the ghost . . .*

Rebecca shook Adam out of his daydream. "Are you okay?"

"Yeah, sure. What did Lilly mean when she said 'find Bill's ring'?"

"You'll have to ask her about that. It looks like they have things under control. This might be a good time to go back to the dining room and see how your mom is doing in the kitchen. I hear she's a great cook, and I'm dying to taste her food."

"Rebecca?"

"Yes, Adam?"

"Please let's not talk about ghosts or dying over lunch."

"Sure, Adam." She picked up her phone. "Let me just phone the kitchen to let them know we're on our way."

CHAPTER SIX

STU AND JACK STEPPED OFF THE ELEVATOR, CARTING SOME OXYGEN TANKS. A few of the memory care staff were still attending to Lilly.

"What's goin' on?" asked Stu.

"Lilly fell again," said one of the staff.

"Did she get hurt?"

"Contusion on her forehead; she's slightly concussive. We called the doctor."

"Does she need oxygen?" Jack asked.

"She's been on it all night. But you know Lilly: she's always pulling off the nose tubes."

Stu checked Lilly's oxygen tank.

"That's odd. It's empty. She couldn't have used it all."

"There could be a leak. It wouldn't be the first time this has happened," the staff member said.

"You're right about that," Stu replied. "But these tanks are sealed units, top of the line. It shouldn't happen at all!"

Stu had Jack replace Lilly's old tank with a fresh one.

"Maybe they should place me in this memory care unit," he said to Jack. "I could have sworn that I replaced her tank three days ago."

"Is it possible that we have defective tanks?" Jack asked.

"I doubt it," Stu replied. "We have an outside service that delivers fresh tanks every day and sometimes in the evening, mostly by Richie, one of their employees. They are very reputable."

"Maybe the ghost is using the oxygen," Jack joked. "Can you picture that—a ghost wearing an oxygen mask?"

Stu thought about that for a moment and quickly dismissed it.

A smile crept across Jack's face.

"What's with the smile?" Stu asked.

Jack replied, "I noticed you have a security office in the sub-basement. When we are finished up here why don't we go check the security-camera system's video files? Maybe we can see this oxygen-breathing ghost!"

CHAPTER SEVEN

THEY SAT AT A LITTLE SQUARE TABLE WITH A WHITE TABLECLOTH DRAPED OVER THE SIDES. Adam's mother gently placed two magnificently plated grilled cheese sandwiches in front of them. Accompanying the sandwiches were two cups of steaming, fragrant tomato soup.

"Wow," said Rebecca, "this looks and smells amazing!"

Adam couldn't wait for Rebecca to taste it.

Adam's mom sat down to join them. "What are you waiting for? Go on, tell me what you think!"

Rebecca took a bite. "Oh my God, this is the best grilled cheese I ever tasted. What's your secret?"

"Mayonnaise!"

"Mayonnaise?" Rebecca asked.

"Yep! Just spread mayonnaise on the outside of the bread. When you grill the sandwich the mayonnaise causes the bread to turn golden brown and makes the cheese melt better."

"Try the soup," Adam said to Rebecca.

After one spoonful Rebecca was convinced that the Smith family was definitely going to improve things at Sheppard's Inn.

"So tell me, Adam, how is your day going?" his mom asked.

Rebecca looked at Adam as he took a deep breath.

He began, "People were screaming, we had to run, I learned about this proximity-door thing, a woman crashed to the floor, she has this bluish-green golf ball growing on her head, she almost died, there was this ghost who I think took Bill's ring. Oh, everyone is in a wheelchair or has a walker, and I am no longer going to eat SuperBurgers and fries!"

Astonished, Adam's mom turned to Rebecca and asked, "Is this true?"

Rebecca smiled and replied, "Adam told me not to talk about it."

Chapter Eight

Stu reached out and opened the door that led to the security room.

Surprised to see that the knob turned freely, Jack asked, "That door isn't locked?"

"The lock doesn't work anymore," Stu replied sheepishly. "It hasn't worked for weeks. Besides, why does it matter? Until now I'm the only one who is ever down here. Maybe that could be your next job—fix the lock!"

They entered the room. Four thirty-two-inch monitors were mounted on the far wall. There was a computer server sitting in the corner next to a patch-panel tower. Below the monitors was a long metal desk with keyboards connected to four large boxes. Each box had a bundle of wires connected in the rear.

"Welcome to Sheppard's Inn Studios!" Stu announced.

"Impressive," Jack replied. "Looks like you have four DVRs, each capable of having sixteen connected cameras. The monitors don't look like they have HDMI inputs. You probably don't have HD. Are the cameras analog, IP, or TVI?"

Stu had absolutely no idea what Jack was talking about. It was as if Jack were speaking another language.

"How about PTZ? Do you have that?" Jack asked.

"Isn't that what a soldier gets, that post-traumatic stress thing?"

"Not PTSD, PTZ. You know—pan, tilt, and zoom," Jack explained.

"Ah, yes, pan, tilt, and zoom." Stu still had no idea what Jack was talking about. "Nope, don't think we do!"

Jack proceeded to crack his knuckles and then let his fingers fly across the keyboards. "Looks like you have old-style analog cameras. They have a lower resolution, which is problematic. You realize that they pixelate when you try to digitally zoom?"

"Hey, Jack, did you once own a security company, or were you a cop or hacker or somethin'?"

Jack smiled. "I've done a little hacking in my days." Jack realized that he would have to downplay his knowledge of security surveillance, which he had learned while taking advanced classes in the police department.

"You look like you can do a little more than hacking. You seem to know a lot about this security equipment."

"Shhh. Don't discuss that with my son. You know how kids are. He'll tell you I was some kind of a detective in another life!"

"Sure, no problem," Stu replied, "Besides, I don't think that Jack Smith is a very good name for a detective anyway. So tell me, Jack, what can you do with all this electronic recordin' stuff?"

"Well, let's try to go back twenty-four hours, and then I'll fast-forward everything at four times the real-time speed."

"Sure, Jack, whatever you say. Let's do that!"

The monitors showed people dashing about at super speed. It was like watching a crazy cartoon. Little clocks at the bottom of the screens indicated that time was moving faster and faster. Suddenly, at two a.m., everything went fuzzy.

"What just happened?" asked Stu.

Jack was perplexed. He went backward and then forward again. There was nothing but wavy lines from two a.m. to five a.m.

"What are all those wavy lines?" Stu questioned.

"Maybe your ghost," Jack replied.

"You're kiddin', right?"

"Nope, there is something happening during those time frames. Something we're not supposed to see," Jack answered.

"What do we do now?"

"Speak to my son. He's the smart one in the family!"

"He's smarter than you?"

"Trust me, when my son is challenged he can figure anything out, and I know that for a fact!"

Chapter Nine

THE SUN SET EARLY, AND THE SNOW FALLING ON THE LANDSCAPED GROUND MADE IT EASY TO SEE THE FULL MOON'S REFLECTION OFF THE SHINY WHITE SURFACES. The outside temperature dropped to five degrees, which further taxed the heating system at Sheppard's Inn.

By ten p.m. most of those huddled by the cozy fire located in the large sitting room began their journey back to their bedrooms. Some of the staff members were busy transporting wheelchaired residents. Others proceeded with canes and walkers, leaving little trail marks on the floor. Televisions were set to favorite channels. The staff adjusted the room timers that would automatically turn off the TVs and lights after sixty minutes.

By two a.m. no activity could be observed by anyone, and that also included any recorded images being captured by the inn's camera system.

Jack and Carol could be found in their small room, lying across their bed. Carol dreamed of her creations for tomorrow's menu, while Jack subconsciously worked out his surveillance plans. Adam was in his closet-like room without a TV, tossing and turning, hoping to finally drift off into his subconsciously created dream world. It didn't take long before he found himself drifting out of the real world.

He was walking outside. There was snow covering the ground, but Adam did not feel its moisture or chilly bite. A large gold Lincoln Continental glided its way from the parking lot and pulled alongside him. Without making a sound, the passenger window lowered, and a man asked Adam to join him inside the luxury vehicle.

"Wow, this is some big car," Adam remarked as he entered and sat on the overstuffed, soft leather seat.

"They don't make them like this anymore," the man answered in a pleasant tone.

Adam studied the man's face. It was a kind face. The man appeared to be too small for such a big car. What was most striking was the man's abundance of silver hair, which formed perfect layers across the top of his head and tapered to his ears. He was wearing a white silk dress shirt ending in silver cuff links, a beautiful striped tie, a light-blue sports jacket, and tailored white slacks with a sharp crease. On his lap was a hat similar to what Frank Sinatra would have worn in an old Hollywood movie. For an older man he was quite handsome. Some people might even have called his looks very dashing.

"I love her very much, very much indeed," said the man.

"Who?" Adam asked.

"My wife. Her name is Shirley," he replied. "She's waiting for me so we can dance again. You must help me."

"How can I help you?" Adam asked.

"Her ring," he said. "I made a promise to Lilly. I can't find the ring. I can't leave. I can't dance with my wife. I need your help."

"What do you want me to do?"

"Lilly knows. Find the ring. Shirley is waiting. She's been waiting much too long!"

...

"Adam, Adam, are you okay? *Adam, wake up!*"

Adam opened his eyes. The big car and the man had vanished. His father was shaking him while yelling his name.

"Okay, Dad, I'm up, I'm up. Stop shaking me."

"You were really in a deep sleep, and you must have had one heck of a dream."

Adam shook his head and wiped his eyes, trying to revive himself.

"Yeah, Dad, like you said, it was one heck of a dream."

"Well, son, today is a new day. What's on your agenda?"

"I have to go visit someone."

Adam's dad was surprised that Adam knew anyone at Sheppard's Inn.

"Who are you visiting?"

"A woman named Lilly. I have to talk to her."

"Lilly?" his dad asked. "Isn't she the woman who fell yesterday?"

"Yeah, Dad, she's the one. I hope she's well enough to answer a few questions."

"What kind of questions?"

"I don't know. I'll figure that out when I meet her."

Adam threw on some clothes and left his room.

"Hold it, son. What about breakfast?"

"No time for breakfast. Shirley has been waiting too long."

"Who's Shirley?"

Adam was already in the elevator.

Chapter Ten

"WHAT BRINGS YOU DOWN HERE SO EARLY?" STU ASKED AS HE SPOTTED JACK STANDING OUTSIDE THE SECURITY ROOM.

"I want to check something," Jack replied.

"Couldn't it wait till after breakfast?"

"I'll grab an omelet after I check the recorders."

Jack entered the room with Stu following two steps behind.

"Let's see here," Jack cracked his knuckles and began typing. He set the machines to search between two a.m. and five a.m. Once again everything moved in fast motion.

"Doesn't look like anything happened last night," said Stu.

There were no flickering or wavy lines. Everything looked totally normal. Jack played it over again.

"Hold it. What's that?"

"What's what?" asked Stu as he studied the screens.

"Those tracks in the snow by the front of the building," Jack pointed out.

"We must have had a delivery," Stu replied.

"Those aren't truck tracks. It looks like they were made by a big, older car, like a Cadillac or a Lincoln." Jack looked closer. "Do you see the width and the length of the wheelbase? Hmm, by the impression of the snow caused by the rear tires, I would say it was a rear-wheel-drive transmission. That rules out a Cadillac. These tracks were definitely made by an old Lincoln Continental!"

Stu was impressed by Jack's detective skills. "Okay, Jack, you may be right. So what's so strange about that?"

Jack's fingers flew over the keyboard, and the video on the screen went back and forth.

"I'll tell you what's strange about that. The tracks start at the parking lot and end up in the front of the building."

"And how is that strange?" Stu asked.

"Well, for one thing, there was no car parked in the parking lot! The second thing is that there were no tracks leaving from the front of the building."

"So you're saying . . . ?"

Jack turned to Stu. "What I'm saying is that we have tire tracks made by a Lincoln that was not seen in the lot. It was not seen when it parked in front of the building and never made any tracks when it drove away!"

"What do we do now?" asked Stu.

"I don't know about you," sighed Jack, "but I'm going to eat some breakfast!"

CHAPTER ELEVEN

"ADAM, WHAT'S THE RUSH?" REBECCA ASKED AS ADAM TROTTED PAST THE MAIN DINING ROOM IN A HUFF.

"I have to see Lilly!"

"Lilly?"

"Yeah. It's important. I need to talk to her!"

"She's probably sleeping. How about some breakfast? Your mom made me a Spanish omelet, and I have to tell you, it's the best breakfast I ever had!"

"I don't have time for breakfast."

"No time for breakfast? Is that what my son just said?" yelled his mom from the kitchen located in the rear of the room.

Adam grinned at Rebecca and started walking away.

"Hold on," she said and grabbed his arm. "I'm almost done, and I'll go with you to the memory care unit. Besides, you can't get in without my door-access proximity card." She waved the card with pride.

"How do I get one of those?" Adam asked.

"From your father," she replied.

"My father? He doesn't have one of those cards."

"No, but he can get you one. He's in charge of maintenance and security."

"Oh yeah, I didn't realize that. Anyway, are you done yet? I'm in a hurry!"

"Here, take this," his mother said as she came from the kitchen and handed him something wrapped in a napkin. "It's one of my new breakfast wraps. I need your opinion."

...

Adam fast walked to the memory care unit with Rebecca trailing behind. He was in deep thought and barely heard Rebecca's plea for him to slow down.

"Hey, you're going to burn out your sneakers if you continue at this pace. What's the hurry? The people in the memory care unit aren't going anywhere."

"It's Shirley!" Adam stated.

"Who's Shirley?"

Adam stopped, turned around, and faced Rebecca. "She's been waiting too long!"

"I'm confused. Did I miss something here?"

Adam thought for a moment. If he told Rebecca about the dream, she would think he was crazy.

"Rebecca, do you believe in ghosts?"

"Ghosts? You mean real ghosts?"

"Yeah, real live ghosts."

"Well, if they were live, they wouldn't be ghosts, would they?" she pointed out.

Adam shook his head and rephrased the question. "Do you think it's possible for a ghost to exist?"

"Anything is possible, but most of the time, when you apply sound reasoning, science, and logic, you will come to the conclusion that a ghost may be more of a fictional character that our minds create when we don't understand reality. They are simply figments of our imagination."

"But what if a ghost actually talked to you, like in your sleep?"

"I would propose in that case your subconscious was seriously working overtime."

"But what if the ghost gave you facts about things you never knew, facts that could be proven?"

"Well, I'd say you have the makings of a good ghost story."

"Rebecca, using science, do you think that a ghost could exist?"

"Let me think about that for a minute while we rest a bit." Rebecca sat on one of the little sofas that lined the long hallway. "I'm sure you were taught in school that energy cannot be created or destroyed. If we follow that hypothesis, logic would dictate that energy can move throughout the universe, changing its state, transforming, and taking new forms."

Rebecca took a piece of paper and a lighter from her purse. "Here's an example. This paper originally came from a living tree once filled with energy. It doesn't seem to contain energy at the moment." She lit the corner.

"I just introduced an external energy source, and look what happened: the lighter's flame caused the paper to burn, releasing energy to create light, heat, smoke, and ashes. You might even say that the dormant energy residing in the paper became alive when exposed to the lighter's flame."

Adam thought about that for a moment. "So what you are saying is that energy is what keeps us alive?"

Rebecca smiled.

"Here's a question for you, Rebecca: When we die what happens to our energy? You said it couldn't be destroyed but it could be transferred to a new form. Maybe that form of energy could go create the life of a newborn baby or other things. Or maybe, just maybe, it can create a ghost!"

Rebecca realized that Adam had a valid point. He was a lot smarter than she thought. "Adam, how old are you again?"

"Old enough to keep from being captured by mobsters, to find my kidnapped friends, and to actually meet Santa Claus!"

"Excuse me? What did you just say?"

"Listen, Rebecca, there's a lot you don't know about me and my family. One day I might be able to explain everything to you, but for right now it's important for me to speak with Lilly. Do you think you can help me with that?"

"Sure, Adam. But one day you're going to have to tell me this crazy story of yours. You realize that it sounds a little unbelievable."

"Yep," Adam replied. "Just like this ghost!"

CHAPTER TWELVE

"HI, HONEY. WHAT'S FOR BREAKFAST?"

"Don't 'honey' me, Mr. Jack Smith. You come waltzing in here an hour late, and you expect me to feed you?"

"I'm sorry. I was a little preoccupied."

"Preoccupied? Such a big word for a maintenance man. And what exactly were you doing while I was slaving in the kitchen, trying my best to keep your breakfast hot? Between you and that son of yours, it's a wonder why I should cook for you at all."

Jack couldn't tell whether his wife was really mad or was just putting on an act. Being a drama teacher made her very good at confusing him. He kissed her on the cheek and said what all men must say to get out of the dog house: "I'm sorry!"

She smiled and placed a beautifully cooked Spanish omelet on the table in front of him.

"I had one of these for Adam, but he was 'too busy' to even try it!"

"Too busy to eat your wonderful food? I swear, that boy must be going crazy. You're telling me he never ate breakfast this morning?"

"He wouldn't sit down, so I made him a breakfast wrap. He grabbed the wrap and Rebecca, and then took off for the memory care unit."

"When I woke him earlier this morning he told me that he had to speak with this woman named Lilly. She was the woman in the memory care unit who fell yesterday. When I got there yesterday she had a nasty bump on her head."

"What were you doing there?"

"Stu, the old maintenance man, and I were called because of a problem with the oxygen tanks. We brought up new tanks."

"Why does Adam have to speak with Lilly?"

"I really don't know. But I did find it curious that he said something about Shirley waiting too long."

"Who's Shirley, and why is she waiting too long?"

"I have absolutely no idea! You're his mother; don't you know these things?"

"Hey, I'm just the cook here. You're the big detective. You figure it out!"

"Okay, but can I have some coffee? I'm going to need a little caffeine to help me think."

"Sorry, all we have is decaf. You'll have to think without the aid of drugs."

"Decaf coffee, a ghost car, and a mystery woman named Shirley—I seem to be having a great day!"

"A ghost car? What's this about a ghost car?"

"I'll tell you about it if you rustle me up some real coffee."

Chapter Thirteen

"Rebecca, how long have you been working here?"

"About five years. Why do you ask?"

"How long has Lilly been living here?"

"I think she's been here for at least ten years."

"And Diamond Bill? How long was he here before he died?"

"Oh, like Lilly, he was here before I started working at Sheppard's Inn. My guess is that he got here a year or two after Lilly."

They approached the locked door that led to the memory care unit. Rebecca went through the routine of waving her proximity card at the electronic reader, the red light turned green, then Adam pushed the big square button on the wall, and the door opened.

"One more question, Rebecca: When did Diamond Bill die?"

Rebecca put her finger on her lip while her mind worked on the answer.

"I'd say about six months ago. It was a very sad day. He had a heart problem that the doctors couldn't fix. I remember now, it was the evening of March 31, around 11:30 p.m. Diamond Bill had pushed his medical button to summon one of the nurses. When she arrived he told her that, once again, he had some pains in his chest. The nurse pleaded with him to go to the hospital, but Diamond Bill didn't want to bother anyone late at night. He took a nitroglycerine tablet from the nurse and told her that if he had any pains the next day, he would then go to the hospital. The following morning the staff found that Diamond Bill had passed on. He had a smile on his face. Yes, I remember it well—Diamond Bill died on April Fools' Day!"

"He died on April Fools' Day? Well, I guess that explains it."

"Explains what?" Rebecca asked.

"The ghost," Adam replied. "It's an April Fools' Day joke."

"So now you think the ghost is a joke?" Rebecca asked.

Adam looked at Rebecca and grinned. "No, actually I don't. Let's go ask Lilly. I bet she doesn't think it's a joke either."

...

They found Lilly sitting on a comfortable reclining chair, watching television in the sitting room, which was adjacent to the memory care's activities room. She seemed to be half awake and didn't hear them as they approached.

"Hi, Lilly, it's Rebecca. You remember me, don't you?"

Lilly opened her eyes slightly and smiled. She appeared to be somewhat drugged.

"You look so pretty today," Rebecca said as she tried to fix Lilly's hair. "I see you took the oxygen tubes out of your nose again. You know you're not supposed to do that, don't you?"

Lilly gave Rebecca a stern look. "It's making me sick!"

"Oxygen can't make you sick. It's good for you."

"Then you use it," Lilly replied as she pushed the tubes away. "Who's this handsome young man? Why, he looks just like my grandson Justin."

"No, ma'am. My name is Adam, but if you want to call me Justin, it's okay."

Lilly smiled and winked. "Now, why would I call you a name that's not really your name?"

My real name is Adam Simmons, not Adam Smith. Does Lilly somehow know my secret? Adam thought to himself.

"So did you come to stare at the bump on my head, fix my hair, and scold me about the oxygen tubes, or is there some other reason for this friendly visit?"

Adam sat beside her in one of the wooden recliners with padded cushions. "Wow, this is pretty comfortable."

"When you get old like me sitting in a comfortable chair is one of life's great pleasures. You should try the food. We have a new cook who can even make mush taste good."

"I know; that's my mom."

"Well, that's two things your mom makes good: the food . . ." She pinched Adam's cheek. ". . . and you!"

Rebecca held in a laugh while Adam sat and blushed.

"Can I ask you a question, Lilly, if it's not too much trouble?"

"Sure, ask away, but please nothing too personal. Proper ladies don't kiss and tell."

Adam continued to blush.

"Do you know Diamond Bill?"

Lilly's eyebrows lifted, and a smile crept across her face.

"Now, that's a strange question. You ask as if he's still alive." Lilly turned to Rebecca. "Oh dear, my memory isn't what it used to be. Is he still alive?"

Rebecca tried to calm Lilly down. "No, Lilly. You remember, don't you? Diamond Bill is no longer with us."

Lilly tried to rise from the chair. "But he visits me to make sure I'm okay . . . he visits me."

Adam could see that Lilly was getting very anxious. "When does he visit you?"

"At night!" Lilly paused for a moment, put her finger to her lip, and then continued: "He was such a wonderful man. He took Shirley out every Saturday evening for dinner and then afterward he would take her dancing. Those two were like Fred Astaire and Ginger Rogers."

Adam had no idea who Fred Astaire and Ginger Rogers were, but he didn't want to interrupt Lilly's story.

"Everyone could see how much they loved each other as they danced the night away. That was many years ago. Shirley always wore this beautiful purple silk scarf. She would give it to me to hold while they danced. They loved each other so much. She had a beautiful diamond ring; that's why they called him Diamond Bill. It was so sad when Shirley died. He has worn her ring ever since."

Lilly began to shake. Her lips quivered. "Oh, my! The ring is gone. Do you know where it is? Please tell me. Where is the ring? This is terrible! Someone must help Bill find the ring!"

Rebecca signaled Adam that it was time to leave.

"But I have more questions!"

"I'm sure you do, but Lilly has had enough questions for today. She can answer more tomorrow."

"But tomorrow may be too late."

"Too late? Now, aren't you being overly dramatic?"

"I guess you're right, but that dramatic thing? It's genetic, and you can blame that on my mom."

Chapter Fourteen

The weatherman predicted a monster snowstorm that would blanket the entire state of Colorado. Heavy snow fell at a rate of five inches an hour. At the governor's orders, all main highways were now to be considered snow emergency routes, and the public was warned to stay off the roads. The incoming night-shift personnel at Sheppard's Inn could not drive to work and therefore could not replace the exhausted day-shift workers. Stu, Jack, and whoever else was available were shoveling the relentless snow from the rooftops to help prevent any cave-ins due to the snow's weight. Because of the danger, Jack didn't want his son on the roof, but soon realized that he needed all the help he could get. Adam's arms began to ache soon after joining the shoveling brigade. It was freezing cold, and frostbite was beginning to affect everyone's abilities. The building's heaters once again were taxed to their limits.

By midnight everyone was exhausted. Reluctantly, they put down their shovels, climbed off the roof, and reentered the building, hoping to warm their frozen bodies. They assembled in the large sitting room located near the kitchen. Adam's mom transported trays of coffee, hot chocolate, and cookies to the weary, semi-frozen staff as they huddled around the oversized electronic-controlled gas fireplace.

Stu stood, raised his cup, and said, "It better never snow in Florida, or my wife will kill me!"

Suddenly all the lights flickered and then went out. Everybody groaned in the total darkness.

"That's strange," Adam said.

"Not strange at all. Power failures happen at least ten times a year around here," Stu answered.

"Okay, that may be true, but I don't think this is just a power failure," Adam replied as he pointed toward the wall.

His father, mother, and the rest of the staff stared at where he was pointing.

"A power failure can't do that!"

He was right, and they all suddenly realized what he meant. "Look at the fireplace. The fire went out also!"

The room grew silent. This was no ordinary storm causing a power failure. Suddenly there was a crash. It sounded like an explosion. The entire building shook. Then the fire alarm sounded, and strobe lights started to blink. Everyone jumped and began screaming. Something was very wrong at Sheppard's Inn.

A thick fog soon permeated every crevice of the inn. The staff struggled as they breathed the sickening sour aroma that now replaced the normal air. One by one, the staff dropped their coffee, cookies, and hot chocolate. They collapsed to the ground, unable to open an eye or move a single muscle. A loud, ghostly groaning soon replaced the sound of the fire alarm - but no one at Sheppard's Inn could hear it.

...

It moved cautiously through the darkness. First, the people lying on the floor were examined to make sure they were unconscious. Then it traveled silently through the halls to the memory care unit. The full complement of staff members was found motionless at their desks. All the patients lay in their beds in a comatose state. All fingers were checked for rings, the dresser drawers were searched, and the floors under the beds were visually scanned. No hiding place was left unexamined. As the hours passed, the entity continued to move from floor to floor and room to room. The ungodly screeching continued in the background until it was finished.

As the sun rose, the entity quietly vanished. The screeching stopped. The fire alarm was no longer sounding. The building's heater began to work once again, and warmth replaced the cold. People slowly began to stir. One by one they opened their eyes. Some were sick to their stomachs, but mostly they were dazed and confused. The floor of the large sitting room was slick with puddles of spilled coffee and hot chocolate. There were bits of broken cookies scattered about. As the people struggled to rise from the floor, they looked at each other and had the same confused thoughts: *What happened?*

Adam was the first to speak. "Does anyone know what time it is?"

Stu looked at his watch. "My good old reliable Timex says its 7:25 a.m."

"That means we've lost seven hours," Adam calculated.

"How do you figure that, son?"

Adam proudly explained to his dad, "The power went out around 12:15 a.m.—that's when the clock on the wall stopped. Now the wall clock says 12:25 a.m. It must have started ten minutes ago. If Stu's watch says 7:25 a.m. and the wall clock says 12:25 a.m., that means seven hours have passed!"

"Great thinking, son. Now I have something else for you to solve."

Adam loved when his dad challenged him. "Okay, Dad, shoot."

"What tripped the fire alarm? Why did we spill our drinks and cookies on the floor? And what caused us all to collapse and decide to take a seven-hour nap? Most importantly, what happened during those seven hours?"

Adam took a seat and shook his head, trying to revive his mind's somewhat drugged state. Thankfully his dad didn't bring up the subject of why the fireplace went out. The first thing that came to his mind was that everything had happened because of a ghost. He knew if he explained that a ghost was responsible, everyone would laugh at him or think he was crazy. There had to be a logical explanation. Being a police detective, his father would always tell him, "Everything has a logical explanation."

Before Adam could come up with any logical answer, he could hear someone shouting from the hallway: "We're going to need some help here!"

Rebecca grabbed Adam's arm and said, "We have to go!"

They proceeded to run down the hall with Adam's father and Stu trailing closely behind. When they arrived at the memory care unit Stu fished a master proximity card out of his pocket and waved it at the door-access-control reader. He pushed the square button, the door swung open, and they entered.

CHAPTER FIFTEEN

ANGELINA, ONE OF THE STAFF, MET THEM AS THEY ENTERED. Her eyes were red, her hair disheveled, and her demeanor was somewhat distraught. Although she didn't drink alcohol, it appeared that she was suffering the effects of a bad hangover.

Rebecca saw that Angelina was somewhat shaky and guided her to a chair. Once seated, Angelina explained that she was very confused. One minute, she was filling out forms at the desk in her office, and the next minute, she found herself groggy with a massive headache. Her watch indicated that she had been sleeping for hours, which made absolutely no sense. As her headache began to subside, she found the strength to leave her office to make her morning rounds.

"That's how I found them," Angelina explained to Rebecca. "In all my eleven years of being a professional caregiver I have never seen anything like this."

Rebecca gasped as she surveyed the memory care unit. Carts and oxygen tanks were overturned; the floor was littered with trash and assorted liquids, but most disturbing were the staff and patients who held gruesome positions as they lay in their beds and chairs.

"Are they dead?" asked Rebecca fearfully.

"No," Angelina replied. "I did my best to check the vitals of some of the residents. I could use your help to check the others."

Rebecca, having had some medical training, grabbed a stethoscope and followed Angelina from room to room.

"It is the strangest thing—they all appear to be in a deep sleep," said Rebecca. "From the way their bodies are positioned, they look like they experienced a nightmare."

"I agree," Angelina replied. "In my opinion, it looks like they've seen a ghost!"

"Did you say a ghost?" Adam's father inquired as he used his detective skills to examine the room. "Logic dictates that ghosts don't exist."

Adam desperately wanted to tell his dad about his dream of meeting Diamond Bill, but quickly decided that the health of the residents was more important.

Stu attempted to clean the mess. "This is the strangest thing. How could a ghost knock over so many heavy oxygen tanks?" He repositioned the tanks to stand vertically. "Now, that's odd," he said to Jack as he handed him one of the tanks.

"What's odd?" Adam asked as his father took the tank from Stu.

His father frowned, shook his head, and said, "You are right, Stu, this is certainly odd."

Adam was confused. "Am I missing something here? What's so odd about oxygen tanks?"

"This tank weighs about ten pounds!"

"Okay, so why is that odd?"

"Stu and I checked all of the tanks the other day and made sure they were all filled."

"Here's another one," Stu interrupted as he handed a second tank to Jack.

Jack easily lifted it in the air with one hand. "Are they all like this?"

Stu went from tank to tank. "Yep!"

Adam was still confused. "So you're saying that they all weigh ten pounds. Why is that so odd?"

"They're empty!" his father replied. "A full tank weighs more than twenty-five pounds. A few days ago they were all full. There is no way they should all be empty!"

"We better go to the sub-basement to get some fresh tanks. We're going to need them to help revive the staff and patients," Stu suggested. "Adam, Rebecca, and Angelina should stay here in case anyone wakes on their own."

Jack turned to his son with a look of concern on his face. "Don't worry. I'll figure this out."

All Adam could think about was his dream. *Why would Diamond Bill do this? He seemed like such a nice man for a ghost. All he wanted was to find his ring and join his wife, Shirley. None of this makes any sense. My dad is a great detective, but he's going to need more than logic to figure this out. He's going to need my help. I just can't tell him why.*

Chapter Sixteen

As Jack and Stu stepped off the elevator at the sub-basement level they noticed water on the floor.

"Hey, Stu, it looks like you may have a leak from a frozen pipe down here."

"Impossible," Stu replied. "All the pipes are insulated, and besides, this sub-basement is thirty feet underground and below the frost line."

It was a daunting task as they quickly walked and examined every visible overhead pipe.

"Look, it's coming from the ceiling. Is there a bathroom above there?" Jack asked.

"Just your living quarters." Stu snapped his fingers. "Maybe one of your toilets is leaking."

"I don't think it's a toilet," Jack responded. "The water dripping from the ceiling is clear. It must be something else. Let's go take the elevator and check it out."

...

It took over a minute for the slow-moving elevator to ascend one level. While Stu was concerned about a major flood, Jack was secretly hoping that Adam hadn't accidentally left the water running in his bathroom sink. They both frowned as they stepped off the elevator. A trail of water led all the way down the long hallway. Upon further investigation, they found the ceiling leaking at the end of the hall.

As if reading Jack's mind, Stu said, "I guess we can't blame that son of yours."

"I never thought that for a moment," Jack replied with a smile.

"Sure," Stu chuckled. "Looks like we have to go up another level."

...

"Holy Moly! Now that's somethin' you don't see every day."

Jack agreed with Stu as they stared at the hole in the roof and the subsequent snow all over the lobby floor.

"A part of the roof must have collapsed under the weight of the snow. We must have missed a spot when we were up there shoveling last night. I guess that explains the crashin' noise we heard before the lights went out. You were right, Jack, a ghost had nothing to do with this. Like you said, everything has a logical explanation."

"This is only one piece of the puzzle," Jack pointed out. "After calling a roofer we should hurry back to the sub-basement and get those oxygen tanks for the memory care unit. After that, we will search for more puzzle pieces."

Chapter Seventeen

"ARE YOU OKAY?" ANGELINA ASKED AMY AS HER EYES BEGAN TO OPEN.

"Yes. What's going on?" Amy replied as she tried to find the strength to stand. Her legs could barely hold her tiny five-foot-one frame.

"Sit back down; you're still a little groggy. Can you tell me what happened?"

Amy pushed her blonde bangs from her face and tried to concentrate. "I was filling out paperwork; then I heard a loud crash, the lights went out, and there was this smell. That's all I remember." Amy looked around with concern. "Oh my God, what happened here? Is everybody okay?"

"We think so," Adam replied.

"Who are you?"

"I'm Adam. My dad is the new maintenance man, and my mom is the new cook. By any chance did you see the ghost of Diamond Bill last night?"

"What is he talking about?" Amy asked Angelina.

"Don't mind him. He's slightly delusional."

Rebecca grabbed Adam. "Shh, if you keep talking like that, I'm going to personally admit you as a patient! Now go find a broom or a mop and help clean up this mess."

Adam realized that no one, not even Rebecca, was going to believe him. Wait; there was one person whom he could talk to. He walked to her room hoping she was awake.

...

"Help!" Adam shouted.

"What kind of trouble is that boy getting into now?" Angelina asked.

"You stay with Amy, and I'll go check," Rebecca replied as she rushed to where she heard Adam's voice.

"It's Lilly," Adam said with tears in his eyes. "She won't wake up. I think she's dead!"

Rebecca put a pulse oximeter on Lilly's finger to read her blood oxygen level and then grabbed a stethoscope and placed it on her chest.

"Am I right? Is she dead?"

"She's not dead. Her breathing is shallow, and her heartbeat is low. She needs oxygen. Go find your father, and get an oxygen tank here *now*!"

Angelina came rushing in with a machine.

"What's that?" Adam asked.

"It's an oxygen concentrator. It takes normal air and converts it to oxygen." Angelina placed the machine's tubes in Lilly's nose. "This will help her."

Adam used his shirt's sleeve to wipe the tears from his eyes and left the room in search of his father.

CHAPTER EIGHTEEN

FOR THE THIRD TIME IN LESS THAN THIRTY MINUTES, STU AND JACK RODE THE SLOW ELEVATOR TO THE SUB-BASEMENT. Once arriving, they stepped off and quickly jogged around the water puddles that now stretched from the elevator at the end of the hall to the room containing the oxygen tanks.

Jack was in deep thought as he examined the floor while walking the halls.

"All you need is a magnifying glass and an old deerstalker cap to complete your imitation of Sherlock Holmes."

"You make a good point, my dear Dr. Watson," Jack replied.

"So tell me, Sherlock, what's so fascinating about the puddles on the floor?" Stu asked as they finally stood in front of the oxygen equipment room.

Jack reached out and easily turned the door's knob to gain entry.

"How long ago did you say this door lock stopped working?" he asked Stu.

Stu thought for a moment. "At least a month or so. Why does it matter? No one ever comes down here."

"Well, Watson, when you eliminate the impossible whatever remains, however impossible, must be the truth!"

"Do you know all the Sherlock Holmes lines?" Stu asked.

"Only the ones that apply," Jack responded.

"Okay, I give, Sherlock. What's so fascinating about a broken lock and puddles on the floor?"

Jack turned his gaze toward the floor around the tanks. He eyed Stu with a look of concern. "The evidence of water and a broken door lock is elementary, my dear Watson." Jack's finger pointed down near the tanks. "What is my greatest concern is who left these footprints on the floor!" Jack knelt down to further examine the footprints. "Without a doubt, I conclude that a ghost did not make these prints."

"And what brought you to this conclusion?" Stu asked in his best Dr. Watson impression.

"I am not aware of any ghost who wears a size 12 Nike!" Sherlock proclaimed.

...

"Dad, are you down here?" shouted Adam.

Jack poked his head outside the door. "We're in here, son."

Adam hurried down the hall, doing his best Olympic moves to jump over the puddles. "What's with all the water?" he asked when he finally reached the storage room.

"It's a long story, son."

"They need oxygen tanks upstairs now! Lilly almost died!"

"Slow down, son. What's this about Lilly?"

"It's true; I saw it with my own eyes. They put this pulse thing-a-ma-jig on her finger, then listened to her heart, and now she's connected to this oxygen-concentrating machine. You have to help her! She needs those tanks. I think everyone up there needs oxygen!"

Stu quickly loaded fresh tanks on a metal transport cart. "What are we waiting for? Let's go!"

Before they left Jack used his phone to take pictures of the size 12 shoe prints. He then helped Stu load more oxygen tanks, and then they left for the elevator.

CHAPTER NINETEEN

ONCE AGAIN IT SEEMED AS IF IT TOOK HOURS FOR THE ELEVATOR TO MAKE ITS ASCENT TO THE MEMORY CARE UNIT LOCATED ON THE THIRD FLOOR. During the unbearably slow ride, Jack, Stu, and Adam stood anxiously in the car crowded with oxygen tanks, wondering what else could go wrong.

Adam was concerned about Lilly's condition. He hoped that she would recover and her mind would be alert enough to answer a few million questions.

Stu was worried about the weight of further snow lying on the roof. The damage they found might be just the tip of the iceberg. Hopefully, the roofers would arrive quickly before a major catastrophe occurred. And then there was the cleanup he and Jack must attend to before any mold had a chance to grow.

Jack was in deep thought. He surmised that many of the incidents that had recently occurred could have a logical explanation. The power loss during a heavy snow storm, the crash everyone heard coming from the damaged roof, the lights going out and the building's heater shutting down due to the lack of electricity—that could all be explained. What didn't make sense was why the building's backup generators didn't work, why the fire alarm went off, why the fireplace fire went out, why everyone quickly lost consciousness for over seven hours, why the oxygen tanks were being depleted so quickly, and, of course, the mysterious footprints. The puzzle pieces were climbing regarding the ghostly happenings. Even Sherlock Holmes would find this perplexing. Jack knew one thing for sure: there were no such things as ghosts!

Stepping out of the elevator, they were immediately confronted by controlled chaos. Some of the staff were attempting cleanup duties, while others did their best attending to confused patients who were slowly beginning to awake.

Adam was handed a mop and broom, while Stu and Jack were quickly directed to patients who were in need of oxygen.

"How is Lilly doing?" Adam tried to ask Angelina as she quickly walked the halls. She gave a thumbs-up as she disappeared into another patient's room.

Rebecca smiled as she saw Adam mopping the floor. "I see they gave you a job best suited for your talents."

"Beats playing checkers with a bald, toothless ninety-year-old who has bad breath," he replied.

"Be careful; one day you will become that person. You already are showing symptoms."

Adam touched his head to check his hair.

"Not your hair, silly, your breath!" and Rebecca flipped him a mint.

"Do you think Lilly is well enough to answer some questions?"

"I wouldn't count on it today. Remember, this is a memory care unit. Most people can't even remember their own names. Lilly may act as if everything is normal with her memory, but the truth is that she is actually tricking you into giving her information. You can't always trust what she says as being accurate."

Adam frowned. This wasn't going to be as easy as he originally thought. He hoped that when he slept tonight he would have another conversation with the ghost of Diamond Bill.

CHAPTER TWENTY

IT TOOK HOURS TO CLEAN UP THE MESS, AND THANKS TO THE NEW OX-
YGEN TANKS, ALL THE PATIENTS WERE NOW REVIVED. They were up,
dressed, and ready for a wonderful dinner cooked by Adam's mom.

The smells of baked chicken, mashed potatoes, and buttered string
beans permeated the entire third floor. It was like magic. Everyone
forgot their troubles and couldn't wait for morsels of heaven to be
served on their plates.

After discussing the merits of the new cook, it didn't take long
before the residents turned the topic of their conversations to what was
truly on their minds: the ghost of Sheppard's Inn.

One by one, they raised portions of their clothing to show the new
bruises on their arms and legs, which were not apparent twenty-four
hours earlier. They talked about the horrid odor that often came in
the night. Mostly, they argued about how their possessions were moved
from where they had been previously placed on their dressers. Some
swore that jewelry was missing, but most were afraid to register formal
complaints. They loved the staff and didn't want to accuse any of them
of being thieves. Besides, even if they complained, no one would take
them seriously. One of the problems of being a memory care patient
was forgetfulness. The staff would point out that their jewelry was not
stolen; it was merely misplaced.

Their mouths watered as apple pie à la mode was brought to the
table. Now, this was something definitely not worthy of a complaint.

They marveled at the way the vanilla ice cream melted over the flaky pie crust. They couldn't remember the last time they'd had such a fancy dessert. Soon, their memories of things being misplaced and jewelry being lost would be erased.

Lilly urged everyone to raise their teacups in unison.

"I would like to make a toast," she said. "To Diamond Bill: may he dance with Shirley once again!"

The room grew silent as the candles on the tables began to flicker.

CHAPTER TWENTY-ONE

WHILE ADAM TOSSED AND TURNED IN HIS BED, HOPING TO ENTER THE DREAM WORLD AND SPEAK WITH DIAMOND BILL, HIS DAD HAD OTHER PLANS, WHICH WERE NOT AS SPIRITUAL IN NATURE. His detective skills would not let him rest until he could find an explanation for the roof caving in and for who or what had left the water footprints on the floor of the room containing the oxygen tanks.

He gently slipped out of bed, careful to not awaken his wife, dressed, and quietly left his room. Within a few minutes, the slow elevator brought him to the sub-basement. He no longer needed to maneuver around puddles because the water on the floor had dried. He slowly traversed the dimly lit, long hallway. Upon reaching the security room, he cursed the broken lock, opened the door, entered, and turned on the lights.

The familiar glow of the closed-circuit monitors greeted him as he took a seat in front of the multiple screens. Cracking his knuckles, he began to type commands on the keyboard connected to the digital video recorders. Immediately, the monitors displayed images moving backward in time. Within minutes he could view everyone on the roof frantically trying to remove the drifting snow with their shovels. He could see that the spot of roof above the lobby had been missed. That explained why the roof had caved in.

He typed additional commands to move the images slightly forward in time and then switched the view to the parking lots and the roads leading to the front and rear of Sheppard's Inn. Soon, he saw a white panel truck parked behind the building. Due to the volume of snow falling, he couldn't make out the lettering printed on the side of the truck. Maybe it belonged to one of the staff members, or just maybe it could answer a few more of his questions about the watery footprints. While he was using the digital zoom to enlarge the image of the van, he never noticed the parked car in the side parking lot. It was an old Lincoln Continental. One moment it was there, and then it was gone.

He turned on the printer and sent a command to produce a hard copy of the enlarged image of the van. Once he had the picture of the van in his hand he instructed the DVR to return to its normal "live" setting, which the monitors confirmed seconds later.

As he left the room, he didn't notice what had once again appeared on the screen. The old Lincoln Continental was no longer parked in the side lot. It had moved and was now at the entrance of Sheppard's Inn.

CHAPTER TWENTY-TWO

"I'VE BEEN WAITING FOR YOU, SON," DIAMOND BILL SAID AS HE OPENED THE PASSENGER DOOR. *Once again he beckoned Adam to climb onto the soft leather seat.*

"This is really a nice car," Adam said as he ran his hand across the seat and dashboard. "Does it have satellite radio and GPS?"

"Nope, not even a cup holder," Bill replied with a smile.

"But what about your coffee? Where would you put it?"

"Why would I drink cold coffee from a paper cup in a car? The proper way to drink coffee is sitting at a diner, talking to friends. Nothing is better than a fresh cup of hot coffee. You can tell it's fresh because of the bubbles it makes when it's poured."

"Seriously?" Adam asked.

Bill smiled and said, "One day you'll realize how much knowledge old people have!"

"Speaking of knowledge, I have a question to ask you, if you don't mind."

"Go on, son. It's your dream."

"Everyone thinks that you are responsible for what's going on around here, that you're hurting people, moving things around, and maybe stealing stuff. Is that true?"

Diamond Bill frowned in disappointment. "Do you think I'm a bad ghost?"

"I don't know what to think."

"Well, I can only tell you that things are not always what they seem. I am not responsible for what is happening here. In fact, it makes me a little angry to *be accused of things for which I am not responsible."*

"Then who is doing these things?"

"That's your job to figure out, son. And while you're at it, could you please find my ring?"

Tears began to flow from Diamond Bill's eyes. Adam reached up to comfort Diamond Bill, and a teardrop fell on his finger.

"I can't keep Shirley waiting this long. Please help me! Please help me!"

"I'll try, I'll try, I'll try . . ."

...

"Adam, wake up, son. You were talking in your sleep."

Adam slowly opened his eyes and found his father looking down at him. Diamond Bill and his car were gone.

"You kept saying 'I'll try, I'll try.' What does that mean?"

"Dad, there's something else going on around here, and Diamond Bill's ghost has nothing to do with it!"

His father smiled. "I know, son, I know, and we're going to figure it out! Logic dictates that there is no such thing as ghosts. You realize that, don't you, son?"

Adam frowned. "Dad, I never said that I don't believe in ghosts. What I said was Diamond Bill had nothing to do with what is going on around here. And, in fact, he's pretty mad that he is being blamed!"

"And how would you know that, son?"

"Let's just say that kids dream about things that adults will never understand."

"That may be true, but dreams are not real," his dad replied.

"Really? Have you ever sat in an old, ginormous gold Lincoln Continental and felt the soft leather seats? Oh yeah, and there's no satellite radio or GPS, not even a cup holder."

His father was dumbfounded. How would Adam know facts about a car they stopped manufacturing over thirty years ago? He was describing the exact car that could have made the tire tracks in front of the building.

"And, Dad, one more thing: we have to find Diamond Bill's ring. I made a promise."

His dad was wrong about ghosts. They were real. Adam looked at his finger. It was still wet from one of Diamond Bill's tears.

CHAPTER TWENTY-THREE

"HEY, HOW ARE YOU DOING THIS MORNING?" JACK ASKED AS HE JOINED STU IN THE MAIN DINING ROOM.

"I had a fight with the wife," he replied while biting into a freshly baked corn muffin. "She's gettin' antsy about how long it's takin' to leave this place. I keep tellin' her that if she had a job, she'd probably stop thinkin' about the cold."

"Well then, let's give her a job."

"She's a microbiologist. I don't think they're in need of one of them around here. What kind of job could you give her? The only job open, I figure, is for a ghost hunter."

"I was thinking, Stu, there might be some kind of chemical reason that people are suddenly falling into a deep sleep. Heck, if it's a sickness, it might even be caused by a virus."

"So you think a virus is responsible for all of us crashin' to the ground for seven hours the other night?"

"Just a thought." Jack reached into his back pocket to withdraw a piece of paper. He showed it to Stu. "What do you think about this? Kind of strange, isn't it?"

"Looks like a picture of a white van to me. What's so strange about that?"

"It was parked behind the building."

"Lotsa trucks park behind the building."

"Yes, but this particular van was parked behind the building the night of the big snow storm."

"So maybe someone left it there because they didn't want to drive during the storm," Stu pointed out.

"Possibly," Jack replied. "But I want you to look closely at the side of the van."

Stu looked closer. "All I can make out are the letters YGEN. It could be one of the vans that deliver Chinese food or somethin'."

"Does the staff order much Chinese food here?"

"Not since your wife took the job as the new cook. Come to think of it, whenever we did get a delivery it was always through the front lobby. You might have somethin' there, Sherlock."

Jack smiled. He thought he knew what the letters YGEN meant, but he didn't want to tell Stu yet.

"Why don't you give your wife a call? I think I may need her help."

Now Stu was smiling. Maybe his wife, Michelle, would have a reason to stop complaining about the cold and give him a break.

"Sure, Jack, but I have to warn you, she's gonna yap your ears off about Florida."

"Thanks for the warning, Stu. At least I won't have listen to my son yapping about a ghost."

"What are you two burly men talking about?" asked Carol as she brought them her latest culinary creation.

"What is that?" Stu asked.

"It's a Mexican frittata," she replied. "So I'll ask you again—what were you talking about?"

Both men grabbed a fork and gave it a try.

"We were talking about how wonderful a cook you are!" Jack announced proudly.

"Hopefully, you could show my wife how to cook like that," Stu added.

"Your wife?"

"Yeah, your hubby, Jack, here wants to give her a job."

"A job? What kind of job?"

"Yeah, Jack, you never told me. What do you need her for?"

"Shh, you two blabbermouths, it's a secret!" Jack replied and left the room.

Chapter Twenty-Four

"Oh my Lord, it's gone!" Vicky cried out, loud enough for the entire floor to be concerned.

Angelina dropped what she was doing and ran to Vicky's room. She saw Vicky frantically pulling her clothes from all her dresser drawers.

"Now calm down, Miss Vicky, and tell me what's going on."

"My diamond wedding ring," Vicky shouted. "It's not here, it's not anywhere!"

"When did you last see it?" Angelina asked.

Vicky looked down at the fourth finger of her left hand. "It was on my finger. I've had it there for over fifty years. I never take it off!"

"Then why are you searching in your dresser?"

Vicky's body went slack. She looked at Angelina with a blank stare.

"I don't know. Lordy, I must be losing my mind. It can't be in my dresser. It's on my finger. Silly me, I never take it off my finger. Look."

She held up her hand to show Angelina. Her fourth finger had an impression where the ring once sat.

Vicky looked at her finger again. "Oh dear, my ring is gone! Did you take my ring?" She became agitated once again.

Angelina helped Vicky sit on the bed.

"Now, Miss Vicky, you know that none of us would take your ring. You must have taken it off. Perhaps you left it in the bathroom when you were washing your hands."

Vicky started to cry. "Did I tell you it was my wedding ring? I've had it for over fifty years, and I never take it off."

"Don't you worry, Miss Vicky, we'll find it. Just try to relax."

"Maybe the ghost took it. Maybe the ghost also took Diamond Bill's ring. Maybe the ghost wants everyone's rings."

"Now, now, Miss Vicky, why would a ghost want everyone's rings? You don't really believe in ghosts, do you?"

Vicky stared at her hand again. "Oh Lord, my ring is gone! Have you seen my ring?"

Angelina fluffed the bed pillows. "Miss Vicky, it's time for your nap. Come lie down."

As Vicky placed her head on the pillow she said, "The ghost visits at night. It thinks I'm sleeping but I'm not. Terrible smell, but I hold my breath. I'm a good swimmer; I can hold my breath for a long time."

"Yes, you are a good swimmer. Now it's time to take a nap. Can you do that, Miss Vicky?"

"It searches at night. Always searching. Terrible smell."

"Yes, Miss Vicky. You sleep now. Don't worry."

Once Vicky was asleep Angelina quietly left the room. Working in the memory care unit certainly had its challenging moments. She entered the office across the hall, which contained the medical charts, and took a seat next to Amy.

"That was a tough one," she said to Amy. "Miss Vicky claims that someone took her ring."

"Really? That's strange," Amy responded. "Miss Sally said the same thing to me earlier today. She claims that the ghost took it. You know what's really funny? She said the ghost needs a bath."

"Needs a bath? Why would she say that?"

"I don't know. Maybe it smells bad," Amy replied.

"Huh, smells bad? You know, Amy, there's something fishy going on around here!"

CHAPTER TWENTY-FIVE

A TALL, ELEGANT WOMAN WITH SHORT BLONDE HAIR STOOD OUTSIDE THE DOOR. She was wearing three heavy sweaters underneath a ski jacket. Although the door was unlocked, she didn't want to just push it open and enter. Instead, she knocked three times on the outer door-jamb. There was no answer. Cautiously, she entered. Finding a man facing forward at a desk, typing, wearing a headset covering his ears, she quietly approached him and gently tapped his shoulder.

In shock, he quickly spun around. "Holy cripes! You nearly gave me a heart attack!"

"I'm sorry," she replied with a giggle.

Unable to hear her response due to the headset covering his ears, he quickly removed them.

"You must be Sherlock," she stated.

"Who?"

"Sherlock Holmes! At least that's what my husband calls you."

He put a finger to his lips for a moment. "Ah yes, and you must be Michelle," he attempted in a British accent.

"In the flesh." She smiled and offered her freezing-cold hand to shake.

"You look a little cold. Should I turn up the heat a little bit?"

"No," she replied. "What you *could* do is get my husband to take me to Florida. It doesn't have to be Miami; Pensacola would be just fine! Once there, maybe he could start a new career. He could write a crime story and have it published. There's a great publisher in Pensacola."

Jack laughed. "A crime story, you say? That would be interesting. I take it that you are not a fan of Colorado. Either that, or you like wearing sweaters."

"Wow, you really are Sherlock Holmes. Now tell me, how can I help you?"

"Your husband says you are a microbiologist. Is that true?"

"Of course it's true. To be honest, at this point I would prefer to be a chef, like your wife. Standing by a warm oven seems like a much better career."

She looked upon the monitors and other electronics that filled the room and instantly appreciated Jack's ability to understand and manipulate the controls.

"So, did you work for NASA before you took this job?"

"No, I just tinker a bit. My son, now, he's the expert at figuring things out."

"Did he graduate college with a degree in electronics?"

Jack laughed. "Hell no. He doesn't even drive a car. But you know kids these days: they learn about this stuff before they even reach their third birthday. The thing that boggles my mind is that I have no idea who taught them or how they learned it."

"It sounds like your son is pretty smart."

"You would think so, but he has some pretty crazy ideas. He actually believes that a ghost haunts this place."

"A ghost? Now why would he believe that?"

"That's why I need your help."

"My help? I'm not a ghost expert."

"No, but you could help me prove that a ghost has nothing to do with what is going on around here."

"I'll make you a deal under one condition. That—"

Jack finished what she had to say. "That we do this quickly before you freeze to death."

"No," she smiled. "That I meet the son of Sherlock Holmes. He sounds like a pretty cool kid!"

CHAPTER TWENTY-SIX

THAT EVENING, THE MAIN DINING ROOM WAS BUZZING WITH ACTIVITY.
Once it was announced that a special dinner was going to be served,
there wasn't a vacant seat left to be had.

Jack felt like King Arthur presiding over the Knights of the Round
Table. To his right sat Sir Adam followed by Sir Stu and his lovely
bride, Lady Michelle, followed by Princess Rebecca. The seat to Jack's
left was reserved for the queen, who was currently undertaking the
preparations of their upcoming gourmet feast.

"Milady," he said while moving out her chair as the queen
approached.

On the center of the table she placed a large, decorative ceramic
dish covered by a metal dome. Although its contents were hidden, the
aroma couldn't be contained by an elegant yet simple lid. Each diner
sat impatiently as their mouths watered.

"Behold, my newest creation," she announced. "From this point
forward, I proclaim this to be the specialty of the house."

With the great flair of a magician, she slowly removed the lid and
smiled as a cloud of white steam arose from the contents contained
within. As the steam reached the ceiling, it began to spread everywhere
and took on a ghostly appearance.

She pointed to the ceiling. "As you all can see, we have a visitor
from the spirit world who wishes to join us for dinner." She lifted her
arms and then pressed her palms together. "Please no longer cause

fear in our hearts or harm to our bodies. May you take pity on us and be pleased with what I have presented this day. In your honor I have named this dish . . ."

She paused for dramatic effect. Ten long seconds passed before she continued: "Henceforward, I name this dish the Ghost of Sheppard's Pie!"

Adam was the first to respond. He couldn't believe what his mother had done. With great difficulty, he tried to suppress the giggles that soon became uncontrollable, but his laughter quickly became contagious, affecting those around him. Soon, the entire dining room had joined in raucous celebration.

For a short moment in time there were no thoughts of strange noises and horrible smells. Missing jewelry was no longer a concern. The building's heater was no longer problematic but was providing warmth from the bitter cold. Aside from the candles that decorated the tables, there were no flickering lights.

Everyone filled their bellies with the newly created culinary masterpiece. Before long, not a single morsel remained. Life was good.

...

After dinner some people spent time complimenting Adam's mom. Others assisted in the cleanup, while most retired to the community room to watch television. Rebecca walked Adam to the memory care unit, explaining his required assistance with a scheduled nightly social event specifically designed for dementia patients.

Jack remained at the table, drinking coffee with Stu and Michelle.

"So my wife says you need her to figure out what's goin' on around here. Somethin' about its not being due to a ghost?"

Jack had to be careful with his answer. He didn't want to expose too much of his detective skills. Stu had shown his suspicions about Jack's former life. Truth be told, Jack had made a list of ideas and potential suspects for what was happening. Logic dictated that a ghost would be at the list's bottom. The middle of the list was some of the staff of Sheppard's Inn. The top was reserved for what were considered prime suspects. At this particular moment there was only one prime suspect . . . and that was Stu. As the maintenance man, Stu had access to the oxygen tanks, the building's heating, lighting, and, most importantly, the security systems.

Asking for Michelle's help was very risky. It was possible that she and Stu were collaborating. Once they moved to Florida it would be difficult to gather additional evidence. Jack had to keep his eye on them, which required giving Michelle a job for the next few weeks. There was an old saying, "Keep your friends close and your enemies closer." That's exactly what Jack planned to do.

Using a friendly tone, Jack began addressing Stu's question.

"I'm sure we can all agree that ghosts don't exist. Now, I realize that my son would argue that fact; however, I propose that we should assume that the strange events we are experiencing are more likely to have another explanation."

"So what's that have to do with my wife?" Stu asked.

"Well, I was thinking, what was it that caused us to black out for over seven hours the other night? Now, I'm no expert, but it seems to me that many of the residents are also experiencing strange medical problems."

"You realize that I'm not a doctor," Michelle added.

"Yes, that may be true, but doctors only look at the individual patient. I think this is more like a controlled man-made epidemic."

Michelle looked at Jack as if he were crazy. "A controlled epidemic? Seriously, I'd rather believe in ghosts."

"Yeah, Jack, what makes you think it's man-made and controlled?" asked Stu.

Jack realized that he might have given out too much information. Luckily, his wife approached with a plate of freshly baked Danish.

"Do you want to continue to spend time gabbing, or would you like to try my Danish?" she asked.

After taking one bite, the only thing left to say was "thank you!"

Chapter Twenty-Seven

....

ADAM'S ARMS BEGAN TO ACHE, AS HE AND REBECCA HAD SPENT THE LAST HOUR HOLDING UP FLASH CARDS. Each card contained a picture that a memory care patient had to name. What was difficult for Adam to understand was how all the residents appeared to be perfectly normal. They truly enjoyed playing the flash-card game even though it was blatant therapy for their brains. He recalled the good times of family nights when he and his parents would visit his grandparents to play Monopoly. It was odd that, aside from being old and complaining of aches and pains, most of the residents sitting at the table were like happy children. It was difficult to comprehend.

"Rebecca, what causes an older person to become so forgetful?" he asked.

"That's a complicated question. I'll start out with some simple explanations. Many people are forgetful because they get distracted and stop paying attention. Did you ever lose something? Simply put: you didn't really lose it; you just didn't pay attention to where you last put it."

Adam wanted to respond with a big *duh*, but he continued to listen.

"The brain is like a muscle. When it isn't being used or stimulated, it atrophies."

"Atrophies? Is that like it gets sick?" Adam asked.

"It's more like it weakens. Imagine if you break your arm and it is in a cast for six weeks. When the cast is removed your arm is weak, and you have to exercise it to make it stronger."

"Is that what we are doing with these flash cards—we are making their brains stronger?"

"Exactly!" Rebecca replied.

"So if we continue, everyone's brains will get better, just like a broken arm?"

"No, Adam, sadly it's just a temporary solution. You see, there are also other reasons why older people lose their memories. Some are caused by emotional problems, and certainly there are medical reasons."

"Emotional reasons?"

"Yes. Some live in the past, where they experienced happier times. Their brains don't want to deal with the death of a loved one or today's realities, which, unfortunately, makes them sad. They don't understand the technology world of today. It's hard to believe, but, in reality, they have become the forgotten generation. That's why it's so important for them to have visitors who show them that they are still loved and give them a continued purpose to live."

Adam wondered if he was going to be sad when he got old.

"But you said there are medical reasons. Does that mean doctors can cure them?"

"There's a theory that the neurons, or nerve cells, in the brains of older people have problems sending signals because of plaque buildup. It's like a pipe being clogged. If you remove the blockage, the pipe will then allow water to run. There's hope that with the proper drugs the plaque will dissolve and the brain's signals will resume."

"So what you're saying is that there's hope?"

Rebecca smiled. "You have to believe in something. If you make a list of things to believe in, I think *hope* should be at the top."

Adam thought for a moment. "Then why not believe in ghosts? I think that should be on the list."

"Possibly, but only if you can convince people that ghosts actually exist."

Adam remained deep in thought.

"Look, Adam, you don't really believe that the strange things happening around here are because of a ghost, do you? I'm sure your dad would agree that there is a logical answer for all these strange events. I have a pretty open mind, but, like your father, I would need to see actual evidence that ghosts are real."

Adam looked at his finger that was once wet from the tears of Diamond Bill.

"I'm working on that," he replied.

Chapter Twenty-Eight

Jack and Carol sat on their bed and discussed the day's activities.

"That was a pretty funny ghost demonstration and, by the way, the best shepherd's pie I ever ate."

"Jack, I've been meaning to talk to you about that."

"The pie?"

She jabbed him in the side. "No, you silly man. The ghost!"

"Oh no, don't tell me, you actually believe that there is a ghost of Sheppard's Inn?"

"Well, according to Adam there is a ghost called Diamond Bill."

"According to Adam there is also a Santa Claus. Seriously, honey, Adam has an overactive imagination."

"That may be true, but he's not a liar. He told me he talked to Diamond Bill."

"It must have been an interesting phone conversation. I wonder what area code you use when you want to call a ghost."

Once again, Jack got jabbed.

"Adam spoke to him in person!"

"Oh, so you're saying that Adam found Diamond Bill's grave, dug him up, and brought him back to life so they could have a conversation?"

Jack's ribs took another hit.

"In a dream, Adam spoke to him in a dream. Oh, what's the use? Adam told me you wouldn't believe it."

"Listen, Carol, you married a detective, not a medium. There's enough crime happening in the real world. I don't have time to investigate things that don't exist. Now, I have a pretty good idea of what is causing all the strange events around here, but I'm going to need your help."

"My help? I thought you needed Michelle's help?" she questioned with a tinge of jealousy.

Jack took a slow breath. "I need her help for another reason, but your help is much more important."

Carol smiled. "Oh, Jack, you say the nicest things! What do you want me to do?"

"Be an old lady, preferably one with wrinkles, gray hair, and a bad memory."

"That's no problem. All I have to do is not wear any makeup!"

Jack laughed. "You know, Carol, Adam was right when he called you a comedian. But, to tell you the truth, you shouldn't give up your day job."

"What's my day job—cooking?"

"Nope. It's being the best wife in the world!"

This time he received a kiss instead of a poke in the ribs. Jack turned off the light, and within minutes his wife fell asleep with her head on his shoulder. He closed his eyes and thought about the role she was going to play. There was no doubt in his mind that she could pull it off. What concerned him was the story he was going to tell Adam. And there was one other problem: What would happen when Sheppard's Inn lost its fabulous chef? As Jack fell asleep he convinced himself that there were no such things as ghosts. Covered in warm blankets, he never felt the drop in temperature that occurred a few hours later.

CHAPTER TWENTY-NINE

IT HAD BEEN A LONG DAY, AND WITHIN TEN MINUTES ADAM ALSO HAD FALLEN INTO A DEEP SLEEP. Although his eyes were shut, he found that he could see the big Lincoln once again parked in front of the lobby entrance. Without moving a single muscle, his body easily floated to the front passenger seat, adjacent to Diamond Bill. The pleasant aroma of the leather interior combined with the warmth supplied by the car's heater added to the comfortable experience. Diamond Bill was once again dressed in his dapper wardrobe, which included a light-blue sports jacket over a white long-sleeved dress shirt ending with shiny gold cuff links connecting the shirt's French cuffs. Neatly pressed white dress pants covered Bill's lower body. His small black leather loafers barely reached the car's pedals. After adjusting his Frank Sinatra–esque fedora he smiled, gave Adam a wink, and began the conversation.

"Your mother has quite a sense of humor."

"You were there?" Adam asked.

"Of course I was there. Didn't you see me float from her dish to the ceiling?"

"That was you? Really?"

Diamond Bill laughed. "Gotcha! No, it wasn't me. But I was there."

"I thought you never leave your car."

"Now how would I ever look for my ring if I only stayed in my car?"

"So you admit that you're responsible for things disappearing?"

"I never said that. I might be a ghost, but I'm not a thief!"

"Are there other ghosts hanging around, causing these problems?"

"I can only tell you one thing: those responsible wouldn't be classified as angels."

A chill ran down Adam's spine as he thought of movies like The Shining *and* The Exorcist. *In a quivering voice he asked, "Is the devil living at Sheppard's Inn?"*

"It depends on your view of the devil. You see, son, when some people do bad things they often claim the devil made them do it. Look at it this way: we all have a little 'devil' in us, but good people never succumb to the temptation of doing bad things. Knowing the difference between good and evil is what makes the world a better place to live."

"So what you're saying is that bad people are causing these problems?"

"I wouldn't call them bad people; they are just confused as to what's right and what's wrong. They have yet to learn that there are consequences for their actions."

Adam thought for a moment. "Like setting fires and selling illegal drugs to children?"

Diamond Bill smiled. "Yes, but I'm sure you already know about that!"

Adam wondered how Diamond Bill knew about his past life.

"Your parents are good people and have taught you the difference between right and wrong. Now it's your job to show them how much you have learned. Helping me find my ring will help your father find the people responsible."

He took a small piece of paper from his pocket and handed it to Adam.

The car and Diamond Bill disappeared, and Adam was once again sleeping in his bed.

Chapter Thirty

JACK SUDDENLY SNAPPED OUT OF HIS SOUND SLEEP. Something was wrong. Although covered by a heavy blanket, he found his body shivering due to the drop in temperature. Reluctantly, he slipped out of bed in search of warmer clothes. Being careful not to waken his wife, he quickly dressed and exited the bedroom.

Taking the slow elevator to the sub-basement, he quietly walked the dimly lit hall in search of the heater room. To his surprise, he saw light shining from the crack beneath the closed door. Reaching for the knob, he found it unlocked. He opened the door and cautiously entered.

A shadow passed behind one of the large heaters. Jack picked up a wrench he found hanging on a pegboard and raised it above his head. Covertly, he hid behind a tall hot-water tank, ready to strike. His heart began to thump as the shadow figure turned toward him. He could hear the sound of shuffling footsteps growing louder as they approached. His arm began to ache as he held the heavy wrench even higher.

Suddenly, a familiar figure stepped from the shadows. Jack quickly lowered the wrench and tried to hide it behind his back.

"Stu, what are you doing here?"

"What am I doin' here? I should ask you the same thing. And whatcha doin' with that wrench?"

Jack walked over to the pegboard mounted on the wall and placed the wrench on its corresponding hook.

"I heard a noise and thought I needed this wrench to take care of the problem. You know how I am, always prepared."

"So you were going to clobber me with that wrench?"

"Clobber you? Now why would I do that?"

Jack quickly changed the subject. He was curious about what Stu was doing to the heating system. "So why isn't the heat working?"

"It looks like all the pilots went out. There's a built-in safeguard to protect the heaters from disbursing natural gas into the ventilation system. That's why the gas shut off and all the fans shut down. Good thing that happened, because not only is natural gas combustible, it also stinks like the dickens. The gas company actually adds skunk oil to make it smell awful."

"You said all the pilots went out?" Jack asked.

"Yep, pretty darn strange if you ask me."

Jack wanted to ask Stu many questions but was waiting for the right moment. "So what would cause that, Stu?"

"Got me. Only thing I can think of is somethin' blew them out."

Something or someone, Jack thought. "Can you relight the pilots?"

"Sure, no problem. I'll have everything up and running in a few minutes."

Jack looked at the floor to see if there were any footprints besides his and Stu's. It was difficult to tell because the floor had recently been swept.

"Let me ask you something, Stu. Was the door locked when you came here?"

Stu pulled something from his pocket to show Jack. "Yep, and I got the only key!"

Jack smiled and thought to himself, *Either someone else has a key, or I'm going to have to take a closer look at Stu's midnight activities.*

"Hey, Stu, after you relight the pilots how about we go back to our rooms and grab a little bit more shuteye?"

"Sure thing, Jack, right after I finish cleaning up."

Stu grabbed some spray cleaner and a rag and started spraying and wiping all the surfaces of the heater room.

Jack groaned quietly. *There go all the fingerprints I wanted to collect.*

"Can't you do that tomorrow?" he asked Stu.

Stu just smiled and continued wiping.

CHAPTER THIRTY-ONE

ADAM WOKE TO THE SOUND OF KNOCKING ON HIS DOOR.

"Hey, sleepyhead, are you in there? Wake up; we have a full schedule today."

The knocking continued until Adam struggled out of bed and opened the door.

"You're not dressed?"

Adam sheepishly stood in front of Rebecca wearing his striped pajamas and a stupid grin. "What's wrong? You don't approve of my choice of clothing?"

Rebecca laughed. "It's okay, if I was planning a pajama party, but I'm not. So how about I wait outside while you put on something else?"

Rebecca stood on the other side of the door as Adam brushed his teeth and changed his clothes. It was then that Adam's eyes fixed on a small piece of folded paper lying on the floor. He picked it up and unfolded it. He smiled when he saw what Diamond Bill had given him. Carefully refolding the paper, he placed it in the back pocket of his jeans and joined Rebecca in the hallway.

"So what's on today's agenda that's so special?"

"Visitors' day," she replied. "I need you on your best behavior. No talking about ghosts!"

Great, Adam thought to himself. *I actually have proof that Diamond Bill exists, and I can't talk about it.*

"Let's get moving. Your mom has one of her special breakfasts planned."

...

The tables in the main dining room were decorated with white tablecloths and floral centerpieces. Brightly colored balloons and streamers hung from the ceiling. Most of the residents were seated and chatting with their relatives, while others sat with caregivers. Everyone seemed to be having a great time. The excitement was contagious as they eagerly waited for breakfast to be served.

It wasn't long before the kitchen staff wheeled carts filled with steaming dishes to the table. Oohs and ahhs could be heard throughout the room as the lids were removed. It was a smorgasbord of epicurean delights. Thick Belgian waffles, fruit-covered pancakes, French toast, eggs Benedict, and assorted omelets overflowed the serving platters. Everything was piping hot, and this time the steam rising from the food never took on a ghostly form.

Adam and Rebecca took a seat at one of the rear tables.

"It looks like my mom went a little crazy."

"Yes, she's crazy like a fox. You see, once all the visitors taste the food they will brag about it to their friends."

"That's cool, but it's not like this place is a restaurant. Nobody is going to make a reservation to bring their family here to eat."

Rebecca smiled. "Imagine you had a parent who had a medical or memory issue. Wouldn't you want them to live in a nice place with wonderful caregivers and great food? Your mom's cooking could increase our occupancy by more than 30 percent! A great man once said, 'Never underestimate the power of eggs.'"

"Really? A great man said that?"

Rebecca laughed. "Not really, but I bet some wife said that to her husband."

Adam reached into his back pocket to withdraw the folded paper.

"Do you mind if I show you something?"

"Sure, just don't show me a spider that you caught."

He unfolded the paper and placed it in front of her.

"Very interesting. Who gave this to you?"

Adam was reluctant to tell her the whole truth because, like his dad, she probably wouldn't believe it. "I found it on the floor in my room. Do you think Lilly would be interested in seeing this?"

"It's possible, but I'm worried it might upset her. Why don't we wait until breakfast is over and then talk to her in her room?"

Adam shook his head in agreement.

Chapter Thirty-Two

INCONSPICUOUSLY, JACK GRABBED A CUP OF JAVA FROM ONE OF THE COF-
FEE BREWERS LOCATED IN THE REAR OF THE JAM-PACKED DINING ROOM
AND HEADED TO THE SUB-BASEMENT. Hopefully, the CCTV system in
the security room would supply some evidence regarding Stu's move-
ments last night. He made one stop at the storage closet before reaching
his final destination. Finding the necessary parts, he continued his trek.
In his hand was now a cardboard box containing a replacement lock,
some small tools, and a small dome-style security camera.

It took only minutes to swap out the broken knob lock. Satisfied
that the door could now be properly secured, he placed both of the new
lock's keys in his front pocket. Later that night he would place a small
drop of his wife's red nail polish on each key to help distinguish them
from the collection on his crowded key ring.

He then took a seat at the metal workbench and disassembled
the dome camera. Unlike the other cameras installed throughout the
facility, the camera was an IP unit, which required no direct wiring to
the existing digital recorders. Using the internet, this camera would
send its video to a cloud-based storage server, which could be accessed
by a computer or smart phone. It was important to hide the camera;
which is why Jack removed the one-inch circuit board from its housing
and carefully placed it inside an air-return vent located on the far wall
near the ceiling. The camera had a self-contained battery pack allowing
operation for up to thirty-six hours, which, of course, was dependent

upon the camera's software setting. Jack made sure to program the camera in the "motion detect" mode, which would supply the longest record time. He then enrolled the camera's IP address within the range of the building's wireless router and registered it with the cloud-based server. It took him a few minutes to download the application on his phone. Once completed, he tested the system, and it worked like a charm.

After viewing the images of himself on his phone, he became somewhat disappointed when he saw how large the bald spot on his head had become.

Careful not to leave any evidence, he made sure to place all the packing materials from the camera and door lock into the now-empty cardboard box, which he would take with him when he left the security room.

He moved from the metal workbench to the desk in front of the CCTV monitors. After his routine of cracking his knuckles, he began typing on the keyboard and issued commands to view the video images that were recorded between one a.m. and two a.m. the previous night. The exterior and interior cameras instantly displayed images beginning with the starting point. There was no activity at all. He issued a command to fast-forward events at four times the normal speed, causing the time stamp below the stationery images to quickly advance. It wasn't until 1:45 a.m. that the camera outside the lobby entrance began to flicker with what appeared to be some kind of interference.

Jack pressed "pause" and switched one of the monitors to full-screen mode, enlarging the lobby camera image. He shuttled the time back and forth. For a split second the image stabilized and he could make out what the camera had captured. To his shock, he saw his son standing beside an old car. He couldn't believe his eyes. Adam should have been sleeping in his room at that hour. What was even more confusing was the model of the car—an old gold-colored Lincoln Continental.

The image lasted for only two seconds and then disappeared. Jack sent a command to the printer to make a copy of what he had seen on the screen, but to no avail. He spent the next hour at the keyboard issuing commands to the DVR and the printer without success. Try as he might, the printer would only produce a picture of wavy lines.

Chapter Thirty-Three

After breakfast the residents, accompanied by their relatives, slowly returned to their respective rooms. The staff was pleased to see the positive effect the visitors were having on all the memory care patients. Adding to the party-like atmosphere were the sounds of show tunes being played by one of the relative's son, who had brought a Yamaha keyboard. Many of the residents were dancing with their families, while others were on their feet, strollers in hand, moving with the beat of music from the thirties, forties, and fifties. For a moment in time, pain was forgotten as the music turned older people young again.

Adam and Rebecca watched and used their phones to snap pictures as Lilly, holding her stroller, shook her booty while gliding across the wooden floor.

"They sure look like they are having fun," Adam stated as Lilly danced closer and winked at him.

"I think she likes you," Rebecca replied. "Maybe you should dance with her."

Adam blushed. "I don't know how to dance, especially to that kind of music."

"I'll make you a deal: I'll dance with Mr. Saskin if you dance with Lilly."

Adam looked at the way Mr. Saskin was gyrating his hips and thought, *I wonder if Rebecca could even keep up with that guy?*

"Okay, you got a deal," and he shook hands with Rebecca.

He approached Lilly. "Do you know how to fox-trot?" she asked.

Adam didn't even know how to "fox-walk," let alone fox-trot. "Sure!" he replied.

As the song "Hello, Dolly" started to play, Adam's dance partner pulled him into the center of the room. She began singing, and soon everyone joined in.

"Well, hello, Lilly . . . How are *you*, Lilly? It's so nice to have you back where you belong. You're lookin' swell, Lilly . . . we can tell, Lilly . . . you're still glowin' . . . you're still crowin' . . . you're still goin' strong."

As Adam listened to the lyrics, he wondered if the songwriter had written the words specifically for this moment in time. The Forgotten Generation seemed no longer forgotten as they relived their younger years.

It was hours before everyone realized how exhausted they had become. Even Mr. Saskin's hips stopped gyrating. Both Adam and Rebecca were out of breath from trying to keep up with their dance partners.

"Nap time!" one of the staff members yelled.

Some of the residents booed, as others, including Lilly, reluctantly used their strollers to assist them as they navigated back to their rooms.

Adam removed the paper from his back pocket. "Do you think we should show her this now?" he asked Rebecca.

"She's pretty tired, but I guess we can try."

When they entered Lilly's room they found that she had already positioned herself in bed with two pillows under her head. She smiled when she saw Adam.

"You sure tuckered me out. The last time I danced like that was when I was with Diamond Bill and his wife, Shirley. Now, they knew how to dance. I would hold Shirley's purple scarf as she danced. She loved that scarf, but she never wore it when she was dancing with Bill. Did I ever tell you that?"

Adam nodded his head in acknowledgment and smiled back.

"Lilly, would you mind if I showed you something?"

Lilly began to yawn and replied in a soft voice, "Sure."

Adam unfolded the paper and held it in front of Lilly's face.

"Yes, that's it!" she said. Then her eyes closed and she fell asleep.

CHAPTER THIRTY-FOUR

AT THREE P.M. CAROL AND JACK FINALLY HAD TIME TO TALK. After checking to make sure the dining room was clear of any eavesdroppers, they both took a cup of coffee to a small table in the middle of the room.

"That was some feast you cooked up."

"I could have made more, but I ran out of eggs."

"I hope you trained someone to take your place."

"I trained both Cheryl and Lynn. I left them all my recipes. They should be able to handle it, and I gave them my cell number if they run into any problems."

"So the story is that you have to visit your friend Bonnie because her husband, Steve, was in a car accident."

"Sounds like a plan to me. I just hope Adam believes it," Carol replied.

"I'll handle Adam. You just do your thing."

"I'm getting old as we speak," Carol laughed. She kissed him and rose from the table.

"Be careful, honey. This could be dangerous."

"Now, who's going to hurt a little old bubby like me?"

As Carol left, Jack couldn't help but smile as he saw her beginning to hunch over and walk away with a limp. Now all he had to do was place the doctored paperwork in the administrator's file cabinet.

...

As Adam accompanied Rebecca back from the memory care unit, he spotted his father exiting the dining room.

"Hey, Dad, I looked for you at breakfast, but I couldn't find you anywhere."

"You know me, son—always checking out something."

"Mom really outdid herself. You missed some great food."

Jack patted his stomach, which had grown a bit in the last few weeks. "I could use a break from Mom's cooking."

"Not me," Adam replied. "She's the best cook ever!"

"I'm sure Cheryl and Lynn will do just fine."

"Who are Cheryl and Lynn? What are you talking about?"

"Oh, I'm sorry, I forgot to tell you. Your mom has to leave for a week or so. Cheryl and Lynn will be taking her place."

"Yeah, right, and Diamond Bill is going to teach me to drive," he answered sarcastically.

"Fair enough, but what car is he going to use when he teaches you?"

"His big Lincoln. It's old, but I know I can drive it." Adam continued the charade.

"Just curious, son—what color is his car?"

"Gold. Don't you ever listen to what I say? I told you before, Diamond Bill drives a gold Lincoln Continental!"

Jack remembered what he had seen for two seconds on the CCTV monitor.

"Gold, you say?" He never heard the response as Adam walked away.

Chapter Thirty-Five

Before retiring to his room, Jack decided to go for a stroll in the sub-basement. He checked the doors to the security and heater rooms and found them to be securely locked. Continuing his tour, he looked for places he could hide additional IP cameras. When he finally reached the room containing the oxygen tanks he tried the door and found it unlocked. Hearing the sounds of movement coming from within, he opened the door and cautiously stepped inside.

To his surprise, he found Stu moving the tanks.

"Hey, Stu, I see you are doing a little redecorating."

Stu turned and was shocked to see Jack standing there.

"Just a little organizin'," he stammered.

Jack noticed that some of the tanks looked different than the others.

"I never noticed that before," Jack said while pointing to the tanks. "Why do some of those tanks have blue dots?"

Stu appeared to be very nervous. "Hmm, I just noticed that myself."

Jack thought back to the two keys he had placed in his pocket and how he was going to use red nail polish to distinguish them from his other keys.

"Do you think the dots mean anything?"

"Nah, in fact, some of those tanks were just delivered by Richie. That's why I'm moving things around. I always like to use the old inventory first."

"I wasn't aware that oxygen went bad as it got older," Jack said. "Besides, the way we go through oxygen around here, none of the tanks could be more than two weeks old."

Stu frowned. "I guess you're tellin' me that I'm wastin' my time."

Jack spotted some strange large footprints on the floor and wanted to examine them.

"Speaking of wasting your time," he said to Stu. "Don't bother cleaning up when you're finished. I put mopping the floors on my list of things to do tomorrow."

"Sure thing, Jack. Give me a minute and we will both leave together."

On the way back to their rooms Stu seemed disturbed.

"Hey, Jack, I've been meanin' to ask you somethin'. I noticed that you replaced the lock on the security room door."

Jack nodded in agreement.

"I was just wonderin', were you plannin' on givin' me a key?"

"I didn't think you needed one," Jack replied. "You told me that you didn't even know how to work the equipment."

"That may be true, but until I leave I'm still in charge of maintenance around here, and I should have a key to all the doors."

"I'll tell you what, Stu." Jack placed his hand in his right front pocket. "The lock only came with one key, but I'll make you a duplicate."

Stu knew that locks always came with two keys. Something was up. Why would Jack lie to him? He frowned. "Thanks, Jack."

...

Later that night there was a knock on Jack's door.

"Dad, it's me, Adam. Can I come in?"

"Sure, son. What's up?"

Adam realized that his mom was not there and his father had not been kidding about his mom leaving.

"It's about Mom. You never told me. Is she okay?"

Jack noticed that Adam's eyes were beginning to tear. "It's okay, son, everything is okay."

Adam sat on the bed and wiped his eyes. "Are you telling me the truth? Is mom sick? Because I can't think of any other reason why she would have to leave."

Jack hated lying to Adam, even if it was a little white lie. He hugged him.

"Your mom is fine. She just had to visit her friend Bonnie for a week, that's all."

Adam was suspicious. He and his family were living under assumed names because they couldn't risk being found by the mob. He thought hard but couldn't remember his mom ever talking about a friend named Bonnie.

"What is so important that she has to visit her friend?"

"Bonnie's husband, Steve, was in a car accident. Your mom is helping her out."

"Really? That's the truth?"

"Sure, son. Why would I lie to you? Now, how about I walk you back to your room?"

On the way back Adam kept thinking, *Why would my dad lie to me?*

Chapter Thirty-Six

"WELCOME TO SHEPPARD'S INN," IVAN SAID AS HE MOVED FROM THE LOBBY'S ADMISSION DESK AND TOOK A SEAT ON THE SOFA IN FRONT OF THE WOMAN'S WHEELCHAIR. He lowered his glasses to glance at the contents of the manila file folder he was holding.

"According to my records, your last name is Weiss. That would be Bella Weiss. Is that correct?"

Bella nodded her head, and in a gentle, soft voice she said, "Yes, but you can call me Bubby."

"Bubby it is then! You look very nice today."

Bella, dressed in a pink velour jumpsuit, white sneakers, and a powder-blue shawl, grinned as she fluffed her gray bouffant-styled hair.

"I try to look nice every day. Sometimes it's a chore when you can't find your brush. Do they have extra brushes here?"

"Don't you worry one little bit, Bella—I mean Bubby; they have everything here, including soft, comfy beds."

Her white teeth glowed as she smiled, but not as much as the shiny brooch she wore proudly on the front of her top.

"My, that is a beautiful piece of jewelry," he remarked.

"My husband made it, bless his soul. I never had it appraised, but, knowing my husband, it has great value."

"Did your husband pass?"

Bella didn't want to talk about her husband, so she quickly changed the subject. "You are such a nice man. What was your name again? I'm a little forgetful."

"My name is Ivan. I forget things as well. Why don't I call one of the staff to escort you to your room?"

"That would be nice, Irwin."

"My name is Ivan, Bubby, but if you want to call me Irwin, it's okay. You can even call me Irving if you like."

Bubby smiled. "You're such a nice man. Did I tell you that?"

"Yes, you did, thank you. Oh, look, here's your escort now. Ryan, please show Bubby to her room."

Ryan smiled. He reached for the handles of the wheelchair and gently pushed it to the elevator.

"What a handsome boy you are. Are you married? Because if you're not, I have a beautiful granddaughter for you to meet. Her name is Brooke." She paused for a moment. "Did I tell you she was beautiful?"

Ryan blushed. "Yes, Bubby, I'm sure your granddaughter Brooke is beautiful!"

"Do they have extra brushes here? I'm always losing my brush."

"Yes, Bubby, they have extra brushes, and they also have wonderful food."

"Wonderful food, you say? I'm sure it's not as good as my cooking, so I'll be the judge of that!"

"I'm sure you will, Bubby. Now let's get you upstairs."

"You're such a handsome boy. Did I tell you that?"

Once inside, Ryan pushed the button on the elevator, and it started its slow ascent to the fourth floor.

"You're a ginger, you know."

"My name is Ryan, not Ginger."

"I'm not talking about your name; I'm talking about your red hair."

She reached up to pinch his cheek. "And I just love that cute red beard of yours."

Ryan's face blushed almost to the color of his red hair.

"Gingers are taking over the world, you know. I knew a Shirley once who had red hair. Do you know anyone named Shirley?"

The elevator dinged, indicating it had finally reached its destination.

"Here were are, Bubby: your new home. Now let's find one of the staff and get you settled in."

"Does Shirley live here?"

"I don't know for sure, but I can introduce you to Miss Vicky. She's one of the residents and is friendly with everybody. You will like her. Maybe she knows Shirley."

Bubby smiled. She wanted to meet all the residents and couldn't wait to taste the food.

CHAPTER THIRTY-SEVEN

THE NEXT MORNING, ADAM AND HIS FATHER SAT IN THE DINING ROOM EATING BREAKFAST. They were pleasantly surprised. Although the food was not plated in a fancy fashion, it still tasted pretty good.

Adam appeared to be in deep thought.

"Don't worry; your mom will be back soon."

"I'm not worried about Mom; I'm concerned about the internet."

"The internet?"

"Yeah. Didn't you notice that it's slow?"

Of all the things that concerned Jack, the internet was not even on the list.

"Look, son, you're smarter than me about that stuff; why don't you figure it out?"

Adam grinned. He knew that his dad had more technical skills than he admitted. He remembered how his dad had hacked his Gameboy to store the information that had been used to put a mobster in jail.

"I have figured it out; I just don't understand it," Adam replied.

"Okay, you have my full attention. What's wrong with the internet?"

"It's really a combination of the internet and the wireless router. I looked at the devices connected to the router and found some of them were very strange."

"Strange? How so?"

"For one thing, they were using a lot of bandwidth. You see, when someone is on a computer the data flows only while they are using the computer. Sometimes it may be for five minutes; other times, if they were streaming music or videos, it may be for hours."

"That sounds about right," his dad acknowledged.

"In checking the router, I found other connected devices that send data for less than a minute, then stop and then do it again all day long."

Jack remembered how he had programmed the hidden IP camera for motion only, and wondered if Adam had discovered its connection.

"So what do you think could cause that?" he asked Adam.

"An IP camera programmed for motion would do that. In this case, a lot of them!"

Jack was shocked. He had thought he was being clever by hiding a camera in the security room. Now he realized that someone had been even cleverer by hiding cameras all throughout Sheppard's Inn. The worst part was that he didn't know where these cameras were installed, who was watching, and, more importantly, why they were watching.

"Can you lock out the connections of those IP cameras on the router?"

"I already did that, Dad. I hope you're not mad at me for not asking you first."

Jack put his arms around Adam and gave him a big hug. "How can I get mad at you for being smart?"

"If I'm so smart, then how come you won't believe me about ghosts?"

Jack thought back to the video that showed Adam standing by the old gold Lincoln in the middle of the night.

"I'd love to believe you, son, but I need evidence that ghosts are real. Until then I have to deal with the real world. There are some strange problems going on around here. And I can tell you one thing for sure: a ghost has nothing to do with it!"

Adam grinned again.

"I know, Dad. That's why you have to believe me."

Chapter Thirty-Eight

"EVERYONE, I'D LIKE TO INTRODUCE YOU TO BELLA WEISS, OUR NEW-EST RESIDENT."

Bella motioned for Amy to help her stand from the wheelchair. Once upright she addressed the group in a soft voice.

"Hello, everybody. For as long as I can remember, my family and friends have always called me Bubby, and since I consider you my new friends, please call me Bubby as well."

"Bubby it is," said Amy. "Now how about all of you telling Bubby your names?"

One by one, the residents followed Amy's directions and introduced themselves.

"Pleased to meet you, Bubby. I'm Vicky. What a beautiful brooch you have," Vicky said as she admired the shiny piece of jewelry. "Be careful; things disappear around here. The ghost may take it."

Amy quickly intervened. "Now, Miss Vicky, let's not talk about ghosts. You're going to scare Bubby."

"Oh, I'm not worried," Bubby replied. "I'm sure a ghost would have no interest in my brooch."

"Well, all I know is that my ring is gone. It was right here on my finger. Then, it was gone," Vicky said in an agitated state.

One of the other residents chimed in. "The staff thinks we are forgetful and can't remember where we put our jewelry. That may be true for some, but many of us think it's because of Diamond Bill!"

"Now, now, everybody, please calm down," Amy pleaded.

"We want our jewelry back! We want our jewelry back!" they started to chant.

Angelina came running into the room to help restore order. The ruckus continued until Bubby picked up a spoon lying on a table and started banging it on the metal arms of her wheelchair.

"My new friends, yelling and being upset won't find your jewelry. Why don't you all write down what you are missing? Try to describe your jewelry if you can, and if you have any pictures, it would be helpful."

Angelina, happy to see that Bubby was restoring order, went to the office for writing supplies and then handed everyone paper and pencil. When they were finished noting their losses they handed the information to Angelina, who in turn gave the papers to Bubby to make the list more manageable. She was shocked to see how much jewelry was actually missing.

"Thank you, everyone," said Angelina. "I will forward this information to the police. With a little investigation, I'm sure your jewelry will be recovered."

Unknown to Angelina, Bubby had made a copy of the list for herself.

She paused for a moment. "Oh, I forgot—does anyone happen to know a woman who lives here by the name of Shirley?"

Lilly raised her hand. "I know a woman named Shirley, but she doesn't live here."

Bubby was very pleased with the response. "Perhaps you and I could talk in my room."

Lilly seemed happy to have a new friend to chat with. "Okay."

With some effort, they both rolled their wheelchairs down the hall to Bubby's room. Once inside Bubby locked the door, closed the shades, turned off the table lamp, and whispered into Lilly's ear: "Talk quietly; they may be listening."

CHAPTER THIRTY-NINE

JACK WAS BUSY IN THE SECURITY ROOM WHEN HE HEARD KNOCKING ON THE OUTSIDE DOORJAMB. Now that the lock had been replaced, he made sure the door was always closed and secure, especially when reviewing the images from the CCTV system.

He issued a quick command to restore the DVR to real-time viewing and then went to the door. Once there, he realized that he should have installed a peephole, which would have allowed him to view who was standing on the other side.

"Who is it?" he asked.

He was happy to find out it was Michelle.

"Hey there, Sherlock. You wanted to meet?"

After entering, Jack pulled over a chair and had her join him at the desk in front of the CCTV equipment.

"What I am about to ask you is confidential and not to be discussed with anyone else. Will you agree to my terms?"

"Is what you are asking illegal?" Michelle inquired.

"No, but telling someone could ruin everything."

"And I can't tell my husband?"

"Not even your husband," Jack replied.

"And you'll convince him to take me to Florida as soon as possible?"

"I promise that you will go to Florida, with or without him."

Michelle smiled and extended her hand for a seal-the-agreement handshake. "In that case, you have a deal."

"Okay. First question: If I supplied you with a sample of a chemical compound, could you tell me what it is and what it does?"

"Sure."

"Even if the sample is a gas?"

"Yes, but how would you collect a gas sample?"

"That's my second question: How do I collect a gas sample?"

"You would need some kind of vacuum chamber."

Jack reached into the desk drawer and pulled out a small object sealed in plastic.

"Something like this?"

Michelle smiled. "Exactly like that!"

She took it from him and removed the plastic covering. It was a small syringe similar to what a doctor would use to draw blood or inject medicine. It didn't have the needle attached.

"You see, when you pull back on the plunger it creates a vacuum and draws medicine into the chamber. Of course, without the needle it would just draw air, or in your case, gas."

"So what you're saying is that if I gave you a few syringes filled with gas, you could analyze it?" asked Jack.

"Well, it would depend on whether the syringes leaked or not. I would need testing equipment, like a gas spectrometer, but, to answer your question, yes!"

"Do you have one of those spectrometers?"

"No, but a cheap one goes for around $600 and can probably be ordered from the internet. With a little net surfing I might even be able to save some money and locate a used one. Shipping only takes a few days. Or as another option, I can send your samples to a lab. It will probably take around two weeks for them to analyze them and give you the results. The lab option may be the most economical but will take more time."

"I'll leave that up to you. The faster the better."

"Okay, Jack. But one question: Who's going to collect the samples for you?"

"If I tell you, I'll have to kill you." Jack laughed.

"That doesn't sound like a quote from Sherlock Holmes—it's more like from the CIA."

"Sorry, it's the only quote that came to my mind," Jack explained. "Promise me one thing: when I give you the results of your samples, please don't kill the messenger. Once you get me the results I need, you should start packing your clothes for Florida."

Michelle smiled once again. "I've been packed for two months!"

CHAPTER FORTY

FOR THREE DAYS THERE WERE NO STRANGE OCCURRENCES AT SHEPPARD'S INN. The night of the fourth day, however, proved otherwise. As everyone slept under their warm blankets, the temperature once again began to drop. The screeching sounds were followed by the foul odor that soon spread throughout the building. Those who had jobs that required them to stay awake found themselves unable to keep their eyes open. The lights flickered before they blinked to darkness. Once again the sounds and smells of evil dressed in black moved about the halls.

Bubby lay in her bed, waiting. Her brooch was placed on the night table in full display. Under her covers she clutched the items that had been given to her earlier. Placed in her nose were the tubes that snaked under her pillow and connected to the mini oxygen tank. Her eyes were closed, yet she remained wide awake.

Although she was startled when her door was opened, she forced her body to remain still with her eyes closed. The room was thoroughly searched, and as expected, the brooch was no longer on the night table when the entity finally left the room. It took hours before the odor dissipated. That gave Bubby enough time to do what she had to do. By morning everything had returned to normal. Of course, that was until the residents discovered more of their possessions missing.

...

The following morning, Jack found Stu crouched in the heater room, examining an open hatch that contained some electronic circuit boards.

"Looking for mice?" Jack asked.

Stu appeared nervous and was at a loss for words. "I'm just checkin' a few things."

Jack was aware that Stu's knowledge was limited when it came to electronics, and wondered what Stu was actually doing. He moved closer to the hatch to take a glimpse.

"Do you know what that circuit board does?"

He was surprised when Stu answered: "It's a timer."

"A timer? Why would the heaters need a timer?"

Now Stu became suspicious of Jack's ignorance, but he played along.

"All heaters have timers that control various functions. The best example is how they automatically raise or lower the temperature at different times of the day."

Jack nodded as if this information were new to him. "Is there any paperwork regarding how that timer works?"

"Sure, Jack"—he pointed to a large file cabinet—"it's in there."

Jack took a few minutes to retrieve the instructions and schematic drawings of the timer and carefully review them. Once satisfied with what he had read, he put the paperwork down and moved near Stu.

"Mind if I take a look?" he asked.

Stu stepped aside, wondering why Jack was so interested.

After closer examination, Jack closed the hatch door. He glanced at the paperwork for a second time and then proceeded to put everything back into the file cabinet. Stu appeared very anxious.

"So tell me, Stu, now that you checked, does everything look okay?"

"Yep. All the settings look normal to me," Stu replied without conviction.

One thing Jack knew for sure: the diagram showed that this particular timer was not designed with an antenna for remote operation, yet it was plain as day—an antenna was connected. Jack thought to himself that Stu was either extremely ignorant about antennas and electronics or he was incredibly smart, because there was nothing normal about the timer behind the hatch door.

CHAPTER FORTY-ONE

ADAM WOKE WITH A HEADACHE AND A DISAPPOINTING NIGHT'S SLEEP. He was hoping to find himself sitting in the old Lincoln, conversing with Diamond Bill, but instead everything was blank. It was as if something had prevented him from dreaming. The room had a lingering odor that definitely didn't appear to come from the dirty clothes in his hamper. His brain was a little foggy before he took his shower, but soon after, it regained its sharpness.

He tried calling Rebecca and found it strange when she didn't answer her room phone. After knocking on his father's door ten times, he decided that everyone must be in the dining room eating breakfast.

The slow elevator tested his patience as it ascended to the fourth floor. Upon arrival, he proceeded to the main dining room, in which its occupants sounded extremely agitated. Upon entering he found the staff attempting to maintain some semblance of control. He spotted Rebecca doing her best to pacify one of the residents who insisted in handing her a small sealed package.

As Adam drew closer he could hear Rebecca say, "Don't worry, Bubby, I'll make sure he gets it."

The gray-haired older lady winked at Adam as he joined them at the table.

"My, what a handsome boy. They call me Bubby, and what is your name?"

"Adam," he sheepishly replied.

She reached out and pinched his cheek. "Is Rebecca your girlfriend?"

Adam glanced at Rebecca, and, feeling embarrassed, he stuttered, "No."

"Well, I think you're much too cute to not have a girlfriend," Bubby added.

Adam blushed as he tried to change the subject: "What's in the package?"

"It's something for your dad," Rebecca replied.

"Bubby knows my dad?"

Bubby pinched his cheek once again. "I bet your dad is just as handsome as you."

Adam attempted to move his chair out of Bubby's reach.

"The package contains information she collected regarding the missing jewelry," Rebecca said as she smiled at Adam's predicament.

"I bet all the women here just love you," Bubby continued.

Adam was overjoyed when he saw his father enter the room. With great effort he successfully avoided another pinch as he left the table. He maneuvered his way through the agitated crowd to join his dad, who had taken a seat at the front of the room.

"Looks like everyone forgot to take their chill pills this morning."

"Yeah, and some of them are a little pinch crazy," Adam added.

Jack furrowed his eyebrows as he noticed his son's reddened cheek. "I see you've been interacting with the residents."

"I'd say it was more like being abused than interacting. By the way, there's a nutty old lady back there who gave Rebecca a package for you."

"Ah, you must have met Bubby."

"You know her?"

"I met her. She seems very nice."

"My advice is that you keep your distance unless you want to get you cheeks pinched a million times."

Jack smiled. "Thanks, son. I'll make sure to tell her that you love the attention."

"Great, you're a big help!"

CHAPTER FORTY-TWO

ONCE FINISHED WITH BREAKFAST, REBECCA MADE HER WAY TO THE FRONT, DELIVERED THE PACKAGE TO JACK, AND CONVINCED ADAM TO ACCOMPANY HER AND BUBBY BACK TO THE MEMORY CARE UNIT TO PARTAKE IN THE MORNING'S ACTIVITIES.

Anxious to view the contents of the package, Jack quickly finished his coffee and headed to the sub-basement. On the way he called Michelle and asked that they meet. When Jack arrived at the security room he was surprised to see Michelle waiting impatiently at the door.

"Hey, Sherlock, what took you so long?"

Jack wondered how Michelle had gotten there so quickly. "Slow elevator," he replied as he unlocked the door. Safely inside with the door locked behind them, Jack put the package on the desk.

"So I managed to get my hands on a gas spectrometer. Now all I need are the samples."

"Did you discuss anything with Stu?"

"About the spectrometer, no. About going to Florida within the next two weeks, yes!"

"Two weeks? That doesn't give us enough time."

"It does if you stop stalling and give me the samples!"

Jack quickly opened the package and emptied its contents on the desk. There were pictures, lists, and two padded envelopes, which he gently handed to Michelle. He gathered all the other contents in an effort to conceal them from Michelle's prying eyes.

"What's all that paperwork for?" she asked.

Nervously he explained, "Just a little project I'm working on."

"You and my husband must be cut from the same cloth. He's always working on one project or another."

Jack had his suspicions about what Stu was working on.

"How long will it take for you to get results from the samples?"

Thinking about basking in the warmth of Florida's sun, she replied, "Is tomorrow soon enough?"

Jack couldn't have been more pleased. "Sounds good to me."

"By the way, Jack," Michelle asked, "how did you get these samples?"

Jack grinned. "Would you believe me if I said a little birdie gave them to me?"

Michelle quickly replied, "No!"

Jack patted her on the back and said, "How about if I told you a little bubby gave them to me?"

Before Michelle could answer he escorted her to the door, then went back to the desk to review the papers. Soon he would have exactly what he needed to execute the next part of his plan. He opened the app on his phone to view the images from the IP camera hidden in the vent. To his dismay, it was not working. He then realized that Adam had locked out all unauthorized equipment from the router. It took a few minutes to re-register the IP camera; then, thankfully, the images of the security room appeared on his phone.

Now that the hidden camera was recording and sending its data, the next step was to find Stu and give him a key to the door.

Just before exiting, Jack downloaded another specialized app he needed on his phone and then looked around to make sure that everything was in its place. He was totally unaware of the invisible entity in the room that had been watching his every move. As Jack left, he wondered what his son would think about his plan. The ghost of Diamond Bill, on the other hand, was not so sure and began making plans of its own.

CHAPTER FORTY-THREE

THE DAY PROGRESSED AT A SNAIL'S PACE. Adam suppressed another yawn as he pulled the bingo ball from the spinning dispenser and handed it to Rebecca.

"B-4," she announced in a voice loud enough to be heard by those sitting at tables located at the furthest end of the room. Of course, there was always someone not paying attention who required that the number be repeated; but for the most part, the residents stared at the boards in front of them, hoping to put a little red disk on top of B-4.

More balls were drawn and more numbers announced until finally "Bingo" was called by a happy player. "What's my prize?" she asked as she attempted to move her wheelchair to the front. Adam groaned when he realized that it was none other than the cheek-pinching Bubby. Rebecca stifled a giggle as she watched Bubby maneuver directly toward Adam.

"I want him for my prize," she stated.

Adam was glad he stood behind a long table, which kept him temporarily safe from her grasp. That was until she wheeled her chair around the table and now was only a foot away.

"Help!" he cried out.

It was too late. His cheeks were once again in jeopardy. Luckily, Rebecca came to his rescue before too much damage was done.

"I can't help myself; he's too cute!" Bubby claimed as Rebecca took control of the wheelchair and rolled it safely away from Adam.

"He's not part of the prizes," Rebecca explained.

"Well, he should be—such a handsome boy," Bubby replied and gave Adam a wink.

Jeez, Adam thought to himself, *I'm safer when I'm dealing with ghosts.*

The rest of the afternoon progressed without incident until dinner was announced.

...

The main dining room was once again filled to capacity. Many of the residents talked about bingo, while others complained about the subtle differences in the food, which weren't really about the taste but rather the presentation. Adam groaned when he found his father, who, unfortunately, was sitting across from Bubby.

"There's my little bubbula," she said as Adam approached. "Here, come sit next to me."

Reluctantly, he took a seat at the table and smiled without showing too much interest. He tried edging his chair away from Bubby's reach, but his cheeks were still within her grasp. His father thought Adam's predicament was quite humorous.

"I see some of the ladies are smitten with you."

"Smitten? Really? Who talks like that?"

"I won him at bingo," Bubby exclaimed.

"You didn't win me! Dad, could we sit somewhere else?"

His father looked around. "No place else to sit. Why don't we eat, have a nice conversation, and then maybe you and Bubby can go dancing?"

"Very funny. Maybe when Mom comes back you can work on your comedy routines together."

Bubby reached out and pinched Adam's cheek and said, "He's such a nice boy."

"Your cheeks look good with a little color," his father added.

Adam groaned.

CHAPTER FORTY-FOUR

LIKE MOST MORNINGS, SHEPPARD'S INN HAD MORE CHORES TO BE DONE THAN STAFF TO DO THEM, AND THIS MORNING WAS NO EXCEPTION. Jack sat in the security room, studying his overwhelming to-do list, and tried to use logic to prioritize. He was not expecting any visitors, let alone one at eight a.m., yet there she stood with a big smile on her face.

"Hey there, Sherlock. Are you going to let me in, or should we talk out here in the hall?"

In shock he replied, "Michelle, it's eight a.m. I wasn't expecting you."

"Pensacola waits for no one," she replied. "You wanted results? The faster I give you results, the faster I get to bask in the land of warm sunshine!"

"What did you do—work all night?"

"Well, I thought it would be a good time to work while hubby wasn't home."

"Stu wasn't home last night? Where was he?"

"He said he had something to do here. Haven't you seen him?"

Jack had a good idea where Stu might have been, but he didn't want to say. He would have to check the cameras to be sure. "It's a big place, Michelle. I'm sure whatever he was doing was important."

"Not as important as these results," she replied and handed him the paperwork.

He glanced at the chemical formulas and had no idea what they were.

"It looks like Sherlock didn't study chemistry," she guessed with a grin.

"I'm more of an electronics kind of guy. What exactly am I looking at?"

"You got your basic N20 with a little C2H60 derivative on the side."

"And that is . . . ?"

"Nitrous oxide with a form of diethyl ether that had been altered to make it less flammable."

"And what is it used for?"

"A dentist uses nitrous oxide in small quantities to help patients relax. The ether is an anesthetic that has an intoxicating effect."

"These two gasses when combined would do what exactly?"

"In a high-enough dosage they would pack a hell of a punch!"

"A punch, as in knocking a person out?"

"You got it, Sherlock, but it can also be pretty dangerous."

"How so?"

"Ether is pretty flammable. Now, even though this particular ether has been altered, I still wouldn't want to see it near an open flame or anything hot, especially in high quantities."

"So what you're saying is that in high quantities these two chemicals can put people to sleep?"

"What I'm saying is that after fifteen minutes of being exposed to these chemicals you will be a little loopy and then in la-la land for at least six hours."

"You don't say!"

"I do say. I never kid around when it comes to chemicals. And I have to ask you, Jack, where did you collect those samples?"

"As I said, a little old bubby gave them to me," he replied.

"Well, if she's been breathing this stuff, she's going to need a lot of oxygen to recover."

Jack gave Michelle a big smile. "That's exactly what I've been thinking!"

CHAPTER FORTY-FIVE

AFTER THANKING MICHELLE AND SENDING HER HOME TO PACK THE REST OF HER BELONGINGS, JACK HEADED TO THE ROOM WHERE THE OXYGEN TANKS WERE STORED. As he approached he heard two people conversing. Not wanting to be found eavesdropping, he quietly slipped into the small closet adjacent to the storage room. Unfortunately, the thick cinder-block walls prevented him from hearing any further conversation. He decided that it would be best if he just casually walked into the storage room and acted surprised to see two people in there.

As he drew closer to the door he could again hear their conversation.

"What do you mean you don't have any more?" Stu asked.

"I'll come back tonight. Just give me your keys," the man demanded.

"I hate givin' you my keys. What happens if I need them before you return?"

"You worry too much. It was never an issue before."

Jack entered the room. "Hey, Stu, is there a problem here?"

Nervously Stu replied, "No problem. Well, a little problem, but I have it covered."

"Who's your friend?"

"I'm sorry. Jack, this is Richie. Richie, this is Jack."

Jack extended his hand for Richie to shake. "Pleased to meet you. Excuse me for asking, but what are you doing here?"

Before Richie could reply Stu interrupted: "Don't you remember? I told you, Richie delivers the oxygen tanks. Like I previously said, he just started working for the company a few weeks ago."

Richie nodded his head in acknowledgment.

"Pardon me, but I overheard you discussing that you didn't have any more of something."

Stu interrupted once again: "Yeah, he's out of oxygen tanks. Can you believe that?"

Actually, Jack didn't believe it at all. If Richie didn't have any tanks, then what was he doing here? Also, it didn't make any sense for Stu to lend Richie his keys.

Suddenly Richie decided it was a good time to leave. "Hey, I'm just the delivery guy. If you have a problem with the tanks, take it up with my boss. I can come back tonight or tomorrow—it's your call. If you want them tonight, I'm going to need a key to get in."

"Here's my cell number," Jack replied. "Call me tonight when you get here, and I'll let you in."

Stu was relieved that he didn't have to hand over his keys. "Thanks, Jack. I appreciate that. My wife doesn't like it when I have to work here at night."

"I bet she doesn't," Jack replied. "Now, Richie, how about you go and rustle up more tanks while Stu and I have a cup of coffee?"

"Sure thing," Richie replied as he made a hasty exit.

Jack put his arm over Stu's shoulder. "Let's go, Stu. You and I need to have a little discussion."

Stu didn't like the sound of Jack's voice, but he was in no position to argue.

...

There was not much conversation between Jack and Stu as they took the elevator to the fourth floor and then walked to the now-deserted dining room. Luckily, there was still coffee left in one of the urns. They both poured a cup and took a seat at a nearby small table.

"How long have you known Richie?"

"I told ya, only a few weeks. He's pretty smart, especially when it comes to electronics. Before you came here he helped me with the computers. You know me, Jack—those things are like magic boxes, and it takes a wizard to work them."

Jack absorbed the information and then decided to change the subject. "So, Stu, when are you planning to go to Florida?"

Stu took a big gulp of coffee. "Soon, Jack, real soon. In fact, the wife is already packed."

"I've been wondering, Stu, why are you hanging around? I have things covered here, your wife is packed, yet you are still here."

Stu looked somewhat flustered. "Gee, I don't know; maybe it's because I'm not finished here."

"Well, don't worry. After tonight you will be finished."

"You think so, Jack?"

"I know so!"

CHAPTER FORTY-SIX

JACK DECIDED TO MAKE PLANS FOR HIS NEXT MOVE WHILE WAITING FOR RICHIE'S PHONE CALL. Although it was getting late, he thought it best to contact Rebecca so she could ask Adam to help her deliver Lilly and Bubby to the sub-basement. Michelle and Stu were also requested to be at the meeting. If he had believed in ghosts, Diamond Bill would have also been invited.

Everyone arrived at the meeting place within the hour and was anxious to know what was about to happen. Jack assured them that once he received a phone call the process would begin.

They all huddled in the security room, fascinated by the images captured on the monitors. Soon, one of the monitors displayed a white panel van displaying the word "Oxygen" moving toward the rear loading door. Within minutes the driver exited, walked to the back, and opened the van's rear door. He removed some oxygen tanks, and, using the van's hand truck, he proceeded to roll the tanks up the ramp to the building's loading door. He then picked up his cell phone and called Jack.

Jack asked everyone to be quiet as he answered the phone.

"Hello," Jack answered.

"It's me, Richie. I'm here with the tanks. The loading door is locked. Can you let me in?"

"Sure, I'll be right there."

Jack told everyone to remain in the security room. He would send Adam a text with further instructions.

Both Jack and Stu proceeded to the rear door to meet Richie. One there, they helped Richie roll the first set of six oxygen tanks to the storage room. They returned to the truck three more times until they had transported eighteen fresh tanks. Despite the frigid outside weather, all three men had to wipe the sweat from their brows.

"Well, I guess I'm done here," Richie stated.

"Hold on, Richie. There are some people who want to thank you for all your help."

"My help? What did I do?"

"You saved people's lives by supplying oxygen. You seem to be a very dedicated young man who even takes the time to deliver at night."

Jack then texted Adam to bring everyone to the storage room. It didn't take more than a minute for them to appear. Jack spent a little time introducing them to Richie.

Bubby took the role as spokesperson. "Richie, you have our deepest gratitude for helping us solve our problems."

Richie was a bit flustered and answered, "It's been my pleasure."

With that being said, Jack turned to Stu and in a stern voice said, "Stu, as much as it pains me to say in front of all these people, I am placing you under citizen's arrest. I have conclusive evidence that you are responsible for the jewelry thefts that have taken place in Sheppard's Inn."

Michelle walked over to her husband, slapped him in the face, and said, "How could you do such a thing?"

Stu appeared dumbfounded and angry. "But I didn't do anything!"

Jack turned to Richie. "We got this, Richie. You can go. And while you're at it, you may want to take some of those empty tanks with you."

Richie smiled and selected some of the empty tanks to put on his hand truck. He then made a quick exit to his van, loaded the empty tanks, and proceeded to the front gate.

CHAPTER FORTY-SEVEN

JACK ASKED EVERYONE TO FOLLOW HIM BACK TO THE SECURITY ROOM. Stu protested and proclaimed his innocence the entire way. Once in the room, Jack instructed everyone to be calm and look at the monitors.

"Aren't you going to call the police?" Lilly asked.

"I already did," Jack replied, "ten minutes ago."

Jack turned on the special app on his smart phone and waited.

They all viewed the monitors, which showed the camera images of the police arriving and blocking Richie's exit at the front gate. One of the policemen put Richie in handcuffs and then drove him and the van back to the building's loading door.

Jack told everyone to wait in the security room while he went to meet the police at the loading door. As he reached the door, the app on his phone began to slowly beep. After an interesting conversation, Jack persuaded the policeman to allow him to search the van. Once inside, Jack approached the specific tanks Richie had removed from the storage room. His phone app began beeping so quickly and loudly that he was forced to turn it off. He offloaded the oxygen tanks from the van and used the hand truck to wheel them back to the building.

Jack instructed the policeman to accompany Richie to the security room. When they arrived, everyone except Bubby was very confused.

She grinned, reached out, and pinched Adam's cheek. "Your dad's a pretty smart cookie."

"What's up with you, lady? Quit pinching my cheeks!"

Bubby smiled at Adam and attempted another pinch.

"Thank you all for your patience," Jack stated. "I can see you are somewhat confused as to why you are here. First of all, I wanted you to be present when I exposed the real criminal."

"You mean it's not Stu?" Lilly asked.

"Nope," Jack replied. "Actually, Stu was an invaluable part of my investigation. Without his help and the assistance of his smart wife, I would have never caught the mastermind behind all the strange events happening at Sheppard's Inn . . . including the missing jewelry."

Stu looked at his wife. "You know, Michelle, you didn't have to slap me that hard."

"And you didn't have to bring me to this frigid place to live!" she replied. "I was running out of sweaters to wear."

Jack was happy to see that Michelle's wishes were finally going to come true. Once settled in Pensacola, Stu just might contact that publisher and write a crime novel about what had happened at Sheppard's Inn.

"You can't arrest me!" Richie screamed. "You have no proof!"

"Well, actually I do," Jack replied. He pointed to the tanks that had been removed from the van and brought to the security room. "You see, earlier, when I announced that Stu was the thief, you thought you were in the clear. You were elated when I asked you to take away some of the empty tanks with you." Jack pointed to the tanks that were now in the security room. "Removing these specific tanks was your fatal mistake."

"You can't arrest me for taking empty tanks!"

"Oh, but you're wrong. Only you knew which specific tanks to remove." Jack pointed again to the tanks. "These tanks may no longer contain any oxygen, but they are certainly not empty." Jack reactivated his phone app, which began to beep like crazy. Everyone, including the arresting officer, was puzzled.

"This customized phone application is responding to a circuit board I removed from one of Sheppard's Inn's roaming bracelets. For those of you who don't know, a roaming bracelet is used to track patients who decide to leave the building without authorization. It alerts the security guards and gives them the location of the escaping resident. Now, here's the best part: I hid the circuit board in a brooch and gave it to that woman over there." He pointed to Bubby and watched Richie's reaction. "She placed the brooch out on her night table, tempting you to steal it. You just couldn't resist, and you put the brooch in that tank along with the other jewelry you stole."

Adam looked at Bubby, who was grinning from ear to ear.

The policeman examined the tanks and found that they all had false bottoms, which when unscrewed exposed the jewelry hidden inside.

"You can't prove that I stole that stuff," Richie ranted.

"Actually, I can," Jack explained. He reached into a desk drawer and extracted the list that Bubby had given him. "Officer, I believe that you will find the jewelry in the tanks matches this list."

"That doesn't mean I stole the jewelry," Richie pleaded.

The officer smiled. "I'm sure Jack will be able to supply additional evidence that will further incriminate you, but at this point you are under arrest. You see, when you removed those tanks filled with this jewelry you became guilty of transporting stolen goods."

"Take him away, officer. I know you'll need the jewelry for evidence, so for now, I'll just take pictures of it, and then, after the trial, I'll make sure the jewelry gets back to the rightful owners," Jack said.

On the way out the officer turned and said to Jack, "You know, you are a pretty darn good detective."

Michelle quickly responded, "That's why my husband and I call him Sherlock!"

CHAPTER FORTY-EIGHT

ONCE RICHIE HAD BEEN TAKEN AWAY IN CUSTODY, EVERYONE TURNED TO JACK IN THE HOPES OF HIM EXPLAINING HOW THE THEFTS ACTUALLY OCCURRED. Although he wanted desperately to show his detective skills, he sat patiently and waited to be asked.

Happy to be exonerated, Stu was the first to inquire. "Okay, Sherlock, we're waiting for your brilliant deductions."

Jack looked straight at his son and said, "Well, first let me say this: all the ghostly events we have experienced were not due to any kind of ghostly spirit. I want to make it absolutely clear that there are no such things as ghosts."

Adam looked at his dad. "I agree, what has gone on around here is not due to a ghost, but that doesn't mean there's no such things as ghosts! I—"

"Son," his dad interrupted in a stern voice, "we can discuss that further when I'm finished with my explanation.

"I must say that Richie has wasted his skills becoming a thief. His knowledge of electronics, if put to good use, would have served him well. It's a shame that he ruined his life by making bad choices."

"He stole jewelry using electronics?" Stu asked.

"Yes, and that in conjunction with his knowledge of chemistry made him quite a clever thief."

"So he was also a chemist?" Stu questioned.

"Yes, and also an expert in heating-systems operation."

"Whoa, are you tellin' us that a guy deliverin' oxygen tanks for a living was some kinda genius? I guess you figurin' things out makes you a super-genius detective!"

Jack laughed. "No, I just had good people helping me. Take your wife for example: she analyzed the gas that was putting everyone asleep. And you helped me discover how the heater was being used."

"Hold it. I'm confused. How did I help you with the heater? And what's this gas my wife analyzed?"

"Maybe I should start from the beginning by explaining the ghost-like events. Richie formulated an aerosol that was essentially a very effective knockout gas that could cause people to sleep for hours. It was somewhat flammable, which he addressed by turning the building's lighting off so the gas wouldn't combust when it touched a hot light."

"So that's why the lights went out?"

"Yes. He took care of the lights and then shut off the heater by remote control."

"I get it. You discovered something weird that night when I opened the heater hatch. You found a wire that was an antenna for some kinda remote control."

"That's correct. And I also found strange footprints in the room."

"Wait a minute—weren't there also wet footprints in the hallway from the night the roof collapsed? They were Richie's footprints, weren't they?"

Jack smiled. "I guess I'm not the only Sherlock around here. Now let me explain how it all worked. Richie went to the electrical room to switch off the lights and used a wireless remote to control the operation of the heaters. He then filled the ventilation system with his gas stored in bogus oxygen tanks. He used a portable turbine fan to circulate the gas in the building. The gas contained ether, which caused the horrible odor."

"So it was the turbine's sound that made the terrible groaning noise?" Stu asked.

"You got it. Once he was sure everyone was asleep, which he verified by the hidden IP cameras he installed, Richie went from room to room stealing jewelry and hiding his loot in the false bottoms of the oxygen tanks."

"Hidden IP cameras?"

Jack looked at his son. "Adam helped me with that by discovering a group of devices connected to the wireless network that caused the internet to be slow. As I said before, Richie had a lot of skills. All I had to do was set Richie up and let his greed take him down. Of course, like I said, I had help."

He looked at Bubby. "That pretty lady was responsible for allowing Richie to steal her brooch. And she was the one who collected the gas samples for Michelle to analyze."

Bubby reached out and pinched Adam's cheek. "This cutie helped with the hidden cameras on the internet."

Adam rubbed his cheek and complained to his dad: "Maybe you could tell this old lady to stop pinching. Seriously, could you keep her away from me?"

"You know I can't tell your mother what to do."

"What did you say?"

Bubby pulled off her gray wig and fluffed her hair. "He said that I can pinch you all I want!" She then gave her son a kiss.

Needless to say, Adam was in shock!

Everyone had a good laugh at Adam's expense.

"You know, Mom, you can't keep on doing this to me."

"Sorry, son, but I will never stop loving those cheeks of yours!"

Rebecca realized she was holding the list and pictures of all the stolen jewelry. "Why don't we spend some time matching these pictures you just took to the descriptions in the list to help determine the owners of the jewelry?"

Within an hour everything was sorted out except for one ring that the police had accidentally left behind. Adam had found it on the floor. It was a beautiful diamond ring in a rose-gold setting. Rebecca checked the list multiple times but couldn't find the owner. Adam kept staring at the ring because he had seen it before. He reached into his back pocket and retrieved the folded piece of paper. He looked at the paper, then the ring, and then at Lilly. She shook her head in acknowledgment. It was Diamond Bill's ring.

"Dad, this is Diamond Bill's ring. He told me to find it and give it to a special person in his life, a person who was a true friend and who had helped him through tough times. He told me he couldn't move on until I found it and gave it to her. He also wanted everyone to remember what a wonderful person she is."

He handed the ring to Lilly and smiled. "And he wanted you now to be called Diamond Lil!"

CHAPTER FORTY-NINE

LATER THAT NIGHT EVERYONE AT SHEPPARD'S INN WAS PEACEFULLY SLEEPING.

The lights didn't flicker, there were no terrible screeching or groaning sounds, and the air was free of horrible odors.

It didn't take long for Adam to find himself back in the old gold Lincoln Continental. He was happy see Diamond Bill, once again dressed in his powder-blue sports jacket, white dress shirt with the fancy cuff links, and his snappy Frank Sinatra-style hat. The soft, luxurious leather seats made Adam feel as if he were sitting on a king's throne.

"I'm sure you realize that this will be the last time we meet," Bill said.

"I'm going to be pretty sad to see you go," Adam replied.

"We'll talk about that in a minute, but first I want to thank you for finding my ring and giving it to Lilly. I will be forever grateful to you and your family. I can now leave and join Shirley."

"I guess you can't wait to dance with her again."

"And she can't wait to dance with me," Bill replied.

"I'm happy for you both."

"Thanks, but now I want to discuss something else with you." Bill touched Adam's head. "I was wrong when I said you would never see me again. You see, whatever a person does in his or her life creates a memory. When a person is gone, their memories live on in the minds of the people they touched. If you want people to remember you as a good person, then you must live the life of a good person."

Adam shook his head in understanding.

"Now pay attention, for what I'm about to tell you is something you should always remember. Never let anyone prevent you from living out your dreams. You see, a young person believes that anything is possible until circumstances or an older person convinces him that it isn't. Now, in certain respects, the older person may have a valid argument, but that doesn't mean they can't be proven wrong. We wouldn't have airplanes or spaceships going to the moon if someone didn't follow their dreams and make it happen. You have to believe in yourself and your abilities to make a difference in this world. That's what life is all about, son–making a difference!"

"But it's not easy to follow your dreams," Adam stated.

"You're right. Remember, nobody is perfect, but that doesn't mean you can't strive for perfection. Whatever you decide to do in your life, just do the best you can. Become a memory that will make people proud and feel good that you touched their lives. You've met people who have memory issues, but their lives would improve if people are patient, give them respect, and show them love. Love is a memory that is rarely forgotten."

Adam realized the Diamond Bill made a lot of sense. He reached out and shook his hand.

"Thanks, Diamond Bill. I'll never forget you."

Diamond Bill smiled and said, "Now go live your life, follow your dreams, and make sure to do things in life that will make you unforgettable!"

EPILOGUE

ADAM AWOKE IN THE MORNING, FULLY REFRESHED. He could clearly remember his last conversation with Diamond Bill and realized the importance of living a good life. It didn't matter whether his father believed in ghosts or not. Adam knew the truth, and he would never forget the influence that Diamond Bill had on his life. He hoped that Bill had moved on and was dancing with his wife.

As he pulled off the covers to get out of bed, he noticed a rectangular box on the floor. There was a card on the top, which he quickly opened. It read, "We're dancing again!"

Adam then opened the lid to the box and smiled. He knew just what to do.

...

He knocked on the door of his parents' room. Once inside he handed the box to his parents.

"What's this?" they asked.

When they opened the box they saw a beautiful purple scarf.

"It's a gift from Shirley. She doesn't need it anymore."

Adam's dad looked at him and asked, "Who's Shirley?"

Adam just smiled.

ACKNOWLEDGMENTS

I would once again like to thank my smart, beautiful wife, Sharon, who has to put up with all my crazy ideas and stories. The cooking skills of the character Carol were based upon the magic Sharon often performs in the kitchen. Thanks again to my editors, Earl and Regina, who pointed out how to make *The Ghost of Sheppard's Inn* even better. Finally, I offer my gratitude to those who continue to believe in my dreams and offer their support. Bringing this book to life would not have been possible without the help of my friend Dan Vega and his wonderful support staff at Indigo River Publishing.